# Charmed City:
# Thirteen Tales of the Peculiar and Obscure in Baltimore

Otter Libris

by Michelle D. Sonnier



Printed in the United States of America

The following stories were previously published:

"Bad for Business" Malicious Deviance, March 2011

"The Washer at the Laundromat" Cover of Darkness, November 2010

"The Escape of Baba Yaga" Shelter of Daylight Issue 3, April 2010

"Gathering Luck" Cover of Darkness, November 2009

ISBN: 978-1-62796-000-7

Otter Libris

Please visit us on the web at

www.otterlibris.com

To the Men in My Life

To Jasen:
My husband, my love,
My best friend, my muse,
This book wouldn't be here without you.

To my brothers, Mike and Mitch:
You've known me my whole life,
and you still return my phone calls.
Thanks.

To Dad:
I still miss you all the time.
I hope I've made you proud.

I want to thank Vonnie and Katie,
my fellow writer goddesses,
for all the encouragement and beta reading.

And I have to thank Mishka, who saw the first story
in what eventually became this collection.
She asked why I was setting it in New York when
I knew Baltimore so much better.
And the seeds of this collection were sown.

# Contents

# Master Pinchpenny's Heartaches & Cure-alls

Laney laid back on the scrubby grass on the embankment next to Bill, listening to the roar of the traffic of the Jones Falls Expressway overhead. She wondered if, up in the sky, past the pollution and the reach of the city lights, if there were any stars worth wishing on, any stars strong enough for her wishes. Bill cracked open a can of cheap beer, and she heard him slurp.

"You want another one?" he said in a fuzzy voice, then burped. A siren whistled by above their heads.

"I dunno." Laney's voice was starting to slur. She propped herself up on her elbows, flicking an old cigarette butt away.

"C'mon, you know you want it." He waggled a fresh can in her face. "There's only a couple more left."

Laney giggled and took the can, her pale fingers touching Bill's dark ones. "My dad would kill me if he knew...his sweet little girl, underage drinking." For some reason, the thought struck them both as incredibly funny, and they both rolled in the dead grass laughing. When they had slowed to fitful giggles, they sat up, and Laney cracked open her beer.

"Hey," Bill said. "What's that light over there?" He pointed to a faint green and yellow glow further down the gully under the highway, where it looked like it ended in a culvert intake.

She shrugged and sipped her beer. "You wanna go check it out?"

"Sure, nothin' else going on." Bill wobbled to his feet and offered a hand to Laney.

"My hero," she mocked and stood up on her own, giggling again.

They made their weaving way down the gully, the light getting stronger as they went. Crumpled bits of newspaper and empty plastic bags swirled past their feet, like urban tumbleweeds in the light night breeze. As they got closer, they could hear music that sounded like an out of tune calliope in a dark minor key accompanied by a flat tambourine. They stood at the mouth of the culvert, peering into the glow. They could smell roasted meat that didn't smell quite fresh and did smell more than a little burnt.

"What do you think it is?"

"I dunno," said Bill. "It's all a little blurry."

"It's only 'cause you're drunk." She punched him in the arm.

"Am not," he protested as he stumbled, then hiccupped. "I'm just a little buzzed."

Laney rolled her eyes. "So do you want to go closer or what? This was your idea."

"I thought it was your idea. What do you want to do?"

"Since we're already here, we may as well go check it out." She craned her head and tried to look further down the culvert.

"Okay." Bill nodded.

Laney laughed at him and grabbed his hand. "C'mon, silly."

They walked into the wide concrete culvert into the glow. Laney's skin began to itch and tingle, and her eyes danced with stars. Each breath she took felt like lemonade gone just slightly bad, a little bit of the wrong bite. She could see shapes and figures in front of them, swimming through her blurred vision. Bill and Laney pulled closer together and tightened their grip on each other.

The figures and shapes shivered and shimmied, gradually resolving into a dark carnival midway decorated in red and black and navy blue, peopled by hairy creatures of all heights and shades of skin. There was a man with tusks and skin the color of coals deep down in a fire, and he only came up to Laney's waist. There was another man with bright lime green skin with fangs, and he stood as tall as Laney would be standing on Bill's shoulders. Or at least, they assumed they were men. There was no way to tell if the creatures were male or female. They were dressed in a mish-mash of burlap and sackcloth and what looked like Goodwill cast-offs, stained shirts and torn pants too worn to be sold for 25 cents. Some wore earrings in their pointed ears, and some did not. One even had his massive tusk drilled through for a thick brass ring.

"Don't just stand there gawping, ya idjits," came a gravelly voice from near their feet. "Are ye coming in or not?"

Bill and Laney looked down to see a toad-like little man who came up to their knees, whose cerulean skin and floppy bat-like ears swayed when he talked. In his fist he clutched used paper raffle tickets: bent, folded, stained, and torn. He waved his ragged paper bouquet under their noses.

"Ya wanna buy a ticket in or not?" he growled.

"How much?" Laney asked.

"Whatcha got?" The little man pursed his lips.

"This?" She held out the beer in her hand, the one she'd barely sipped on and nearly forgotten.

The little man sniffed her offering and then showed all his serrated, razor-sharp teeth in what Laney could only assume was meant to be a smile. He snatched the can from her hand.

"Such a generous price for a lowly paper ticket," he warbled. He handed Laney the most pristine bit of paper from his hand, only slightly bent with the smallest corner missing.

"And you?" The little man turned a sharp eye to Bill. "What do ye have to offer?"

Bill held out his can of beer. The little man sniffed it and slowly took it with two fingers.

"Not much left," he muttered. "But I suppose it will do."

He handed Bill the most raggedy one of the bunch, stained with some brown substance and nearly torn in half, barely holding on to any resemblance of a ticket. The little man swept into a clumsy courtly bow.

"Welcome to the Goblin Carnival and Sideshow," he croaked. "We hope you'll enjoy yer visit."

Bill and Laney nodded, wide mouthed, and started to shuffle away.

"But a bit of advice for you, girlie," the goblin called out after them. "Seeing as how generous you were and all. Be careful of your bargains; make sure what you get is worth what you give."

Laney nodded again and drifted into the crowd with Bill. Behind them, the blue-skinned goblin settled down to his beer, smacking his lips with delight.

The midway was like, but unlike, any other midway Laney and Bill had seen. There were games. But what should have been a dart toss involved goblins throwing knives at terrified fairies with watercolor wings pinned to a board like so many wriggling butterflies. The little goblins played the game of Drown-A-Duck instead of Pick-A-Duck using live ducks instead of cheap rubber duckies.

There was food. But most of it was unidentifiable to Laney and Bill, except that it smelled like putrid cooked meat. And there were barkers calling out for games of chance, with one goblin in a battered pork pie hat offering to guess what patrons last ate, rather than what they weighed. Bill started to look a little green under his coffee-colored skin.

"I think I might throw up," he muttered into Laney's ear. "What the hell have they done to that meat?"

"Not here," she hissed. "You'll embarrass me." She dragged him to a quieter spot on the midway, hoping to find a safe haven. But nothing felt safe, and Bill just leaned against her, panting slightly.

"Doesn't seem like that young man of yours is feeling too well," came an oily voice to their right.

There was a three-foot-tall goblin with sulfurous yellow skin and glowing green eyes perched on the counter of a booth decorated in tones to match his skin and eyes. The sign above his stall read, Master Pinchpenny's Heartaches and Cure-alls.

"He's not my man," said Laney. "We're just friends."

"As you say, my dear." This goblin knew how to execute a graceful bow, sweeping his scuffed top hat through the air. "Even if he doesn't belong to you, perhaps you'd still like to buy him something to help him feel better?"

She took in a breath to respond, but Bill interrupted her.

"Laney, don't," he said. "Remember what the other one said. Be careful. I'll be fine." Bill tried to straighten up and look less sick. But she was intrigued and stepped away from Bill and closer to Master Pinchpenny and his booth.

"You can cure things?" she said.

"Well, that would be the 'cure-all' part of my little venture's name," said Pinchpenny as he gestured to the sign with a bit of gnarled driftwood that served him as a gentleman's walking stick.

"What kinds of things can you cure?" She hitched her chin up a bit.

"Laney, don't," groaned Bill behind her.

She turned her head and snapped, "It's not for you, stupid. So butt out."

"Well," said Pinchpenny. "It would be a bit of false advertising if I didn't cure everything, now wouldn't it be?"

When Laney nodded, he continued.

"Whatever ails you, child, I can cure it. It's just the price that varies. The darker the sickness, the dearer it will cost you. But I smell nothing but sweet health on you, young lady. As much as it pains me to say it, I smell no need of me on you."

"It's not for me."

"Not for you and not for this young man? I see. There is a look of need about you, now that I look closely. What is it, child? Tell Uncle Pinchpenny how he can help." Pinchpenny extended his hands. His nails were long and mustard yellow, ending in fine points that looked ready to gouge out an unwary eye.

"Laney." Bill laid a hand on her shoulder. "We should go. This doesn't feel right."

Laney pushed his hand away. "Cancer," she said, stepping right up to Pinchpenny's counter. "My baby sister has cancer." Tears were starting to collect in the corners of her eyes, and her breath hitched.

"Ah, well now." Pinchpenny clasped his hands in front of him. "That is an awful disease. I can help you, child, but it will not be cheap."

"Laney, please." Bill tugged at her arm, and she slapped back at his chest without even looking.

"How much?" Her voice was tight.

"You see, the gift of health is not something you can easily put a price on." Pinchpenny began to pace the counter and twirl his stick in his hands. "And especially when it involves a sweet, young lady like yourself. Things get complicated."

"I'll pay anything if you can cure my sister of cancer." Laney leaned forward on the counter and ignored Bill's insistent tugging on her t-shirt.

"Anything?" Pinchpenny showed her a mouthful of jagged teeth, like a mouthful of broken glass.

Laney swallowed hard. "Yes, anything," she said as she swatted Bill's hand away. "My mother gave me these earrings a few months ago, for my sixteenth birthday. They're real gold."

Laney cupped her hand under the gold hoop in her right ear and leaned in closer to give the goblin a better look. Pinchpenny leaned in and inhaled deeply. He leaned a little closer yet to take a few rapid sniffs. Then he extended his long, snake-like tongue and took a good long lick. He straightened up, smacking his lips and tongue together.

"Yes," he said. "Those are quite nice. Good metal, nice emotion. Your mother must love you very much, child. But I am afraid they are not nearly precious enough for a cancer cure." Pinchpenny began to pick at his frayed lace cuffs.

"Laney, let's go!" Bill finally managed to yank Laney away from the counter and began to drag her, struggling, back down the midway.

"If you change your mind, child," Pinchpenny called out after her. "I'll be waiting here for you."

Laney returned to the Goblin Carnival and Sideshow, without Bill, the very next night. She barely paused as she tossed the ticket-taking goblin a full, unopened beer stolen from her father's stash in the basement fridge. Stuffed in her pockets she had all the cash she'd been saving for Senior Week in Ocean City, $423, plus another $50 stolen from her mother's purse. She still had the gold earrings, plus an antique locket passed down from her great-grandmother and a silver baby spoon that had been her mother's, then hers. If Master Pinchpenny wanted emotion, she would give him emotion. She would have the cure for her baby sister one way or the other.

Just as he'd promised, Pinchpenny was waiting for her. He sat casually on the counter of his booth, twirling his broken pocket watch on the end of its battered chain.

"I thought you might be back, young lady." A corner of his mouth quirked up. "Have you thought about the price?"

"I have $473," said Laney and she dug down into her pockets, then slapped the cash on the counter. "That should buy a lot of cure."

"Pah. I have no use for human money." Pinchpenny waved dismissively over the pile. "You insult me."

"I meant no offense, Master Pinchpenny." Laney flushed and stuffed the money back into her pockets. "What about this?" She laid the silver baby spoon on the counter.

Pinchpenny picked it up with two bony fingers and held it up to the moonlight, turning it to see every angle. He rolled it in his fingers as he smelled it, then stuck out his tongue for a quick taste.

"Yes," he said. "This is quite a fine specimen, but I am afraid, once again, that it falls short of the mark. I might be able to heal a cavity for this, or even banish a case of pneumonia, but only because I like you. I wouldn't be so generous with anyone else." He smiled his unctuous smile again and placed the spoon on the counter with careful fingers.

"What if I added this?" Laney laid the locket out on the counter next to the spoon.

Pinchpenny let out a startled breath, jumping into a crouch on the counter, and snatched up the locket and chain with greedy fingers. He poured the chain from hand to hand and inhaled over it like a starving man would smell stew. His tongue flickered out and caressed the whole of it like a lover. He let out a stifled moan.

"Now, this," he proclaimed. "This is your finest offer so far. The metal is pure. The emotions are so complex, layered. And the age, oh my, it adds a depth I rarely see. For this, I could cure emphysema. Or I could completely remove an addiction, which is no small task, I assure you. But alas, even for this I could not cure cancer. Cancer is far too dark and dangerous a disease." He let the locket slip from his fingers back to the counter, eyes full of regret.

"What if I gave it all to you? The locket, the spoon, and my earrings... would that buy me my cure?"

Pinchpenny cocked his head to the side and squinted his eyes, as if considering. "That is quite a generous offer, my dear. Almost desperately generous."

"But would it be enough?"

Pinchpenny tilted his head to the other side. "Perhaps there is another arrangement we might make, something that wouldn't pain you to give it up."

Laney bit back what she started to say, remembering what the ticket taking goblin had said about making deals.

"Tell me what you want, but no funny business," she said.

"Oh no, my dear," said Pinchpenny, laying a hand over his heart. "I will most assuredly be very serious about this business."

She let out a slow breath. "Tell me then."

"That boy who is yours, but isn't... he cares for you very much, doesn't he?" Pinchpenny smiled.

"Bill? What does he have to do with this?"

"Well," said Pinchpenny. "It's not so much the boy himself, but his feelings for you."

"I have no idea what you're talking about." Laney crossed her arms over her chest. "He's just a friend."

"There are none so blind as those that will not see." Pinchpenny chortled. "The boy loves you, young lady. It's obvious to anyone with eyes to see."

"Loves me!" Laney dropped her arms in shock. "That's impossible. And even if he did, I don't see what it has to do with our deal."

"It has everything to do with our deal." Pinchpenny's voice dropped a menacing octave. "For a pure first love, I would cure your sister's cancer. Give me the boy's love, and you will have what you desire."

"How can I give you his feelings? They belong to him, not me."

"Not so, not so," clucked Pinchpenny as he waggled a finger at her. "He gave you his love, his pure first love, whether you realize it or not. And since it was freely given, it is yours to do with as you choose."

Laney leaned back a bit and ran her tongue over her lower lip. What Master Pinchpenny said sounded so impossible. Her mind juggled the possibilities; whether he told the truth, how Bill really felt about her, and whether or not Pinchpenny could actually cure her baby sister of the cancer that was eating her from the inside out.

"What do I need to do?" she said and placed her trembling palms on the counter.

"Ah, I was hoping you would see reason." Pinchpenny reached under the counter and produced a white brocade box, about the size of an old-fashioned hat box, bound at the corners and edges with brass. He pulled out a slender piece of willow wood, twisted in an elegant shape that echoed the spiral of a unicorn horn and gleamed with an inner light. He shut the box and turned to Laney.

"Just shut your eyes, child," he purred. "And hold still. Be open, and don't fight me when I pull."

She took a deep breath and closed her eyes. Pinchpenny breathed deep as well and drew himself up, arms outstretched like a symphony maestro. He slowly drew a circle in front of her face, then brought the wand down and tapped her forehead.

Laney gasped. It felt like an icy spike driven right between her eyes. But she held still, just as Pinchpenny said she must. He twisted the wand slightly, then yanked his arm back as if he'd hooked a championship bass. When he pulled the wand from Laney's forehead, the tip glowed, and he tapped the top of the brocade box. The glow slipped from the tip of the wand and through the solid top of the box.

Before Laney could catch her breath, he touched her again with the wand, and the pain started anew. Cold fire exploded in her head, and she had to grip the counter, white knuckled, to keep from collapsing. Pinchpenny pulled back and tapped the box to deposit the glow again. Laney clung to the counter, panting.

"Just hold still." Pinchpenny's voice was low and husky and brooked no argument.

His wand snaked in again toward her forehead, and Laney whimpered, but she held still again. She hadn't come this far just to give up. Her knees buckled when the pain came, but she held herself upright using the counter. Something tore deep inside her, and her heart squeezed tight and started to ache. She felt the pressure from the wand leave her forehead, and Laney crumpled to the ground in front of Pinchpenny's booth.

The world spun around her, a jumbled whirl of noise and smell, and greasy blotches of color that refused to become recognizable shapes to her eyes. And her heart would not stop aching. Tears poured from her eyes. She curled into a fetal ball and rocked back and forth. Above her, she could hear Pinchpenny cackle.

"Such a harvest, oh such a rich harvest."

Laney levered herself up and reached for the edge of the counter. Her rubbery fingers slipped off the first time, but the second time, she held on and hauled herself up to a shaky standing position. Pinchpenny had the box clutched in his lap, the edge of the lid slightly up, peering inside, his face bathed in a pure white glow. Laney looked over his shoulder into the box to see what it was that pleased Pinchpenny so much. Nothing was clear in the glow. She thought she saw rings and doves and baby booties. She thought she heard laughter and music and a child's voice.

Pinchpenny slammed the lid shut and turned on her with the speed of a jungle cat. He hissed like a cobra, with his lips drawn back all the way off his wicked teeth.

"It's not yours anymore; it's mine! Get away!"

Laney gritted her teeth against the stench of rotten meat that poured out of his mouth. "You owe me a cure," she whispered.

"Here," Pinchpenny groped in his jacket pocket and produced a squat, square bottle full of a viscous red liquid. "Feed it to the little brat at the stroke of midnight on the first night of the full moon, two nights hence. Now, begone!" He shoved Laney's shoulder.

She stumbled away on watery knees, down the screeching midway, with the bottle clutched tight to her chest, where her heart would not stop aching.

When Laney got home, climbing up the trellis into her bedroom window, she put the treasures and cash back where they had come from. Then she tucked the bottle of cure into her underwear drawer. She got into the shower and turned the water on as hot as she could stand it. She scrubbed her pale skin until it was raw and red, and she still didn't feel clean. She squatted under the flow of water and rocked as she wept. And still her heart would not stop aching.

Laney had no trouble getting her sister to swallow Pinchpenny's cure at the appointed hour. Heather trusted her. The very next morning, Heather had pink cheeks for the first time in over a year, and she ate with real appetite, astounding her mother. The next trip to the oncologist a week later showed rapidly shrinking tumors and healthy liver function. Within a month of swallowing Pinchpenny's cure, Heather was pronounced in full remission. Their mother swore it was a miracle courtesy of Saint Peregrine, and she prayed the rosary every night to show her gratitude.

Laney watched her sister run and twirl in the late spring sunshine in the back yard. She'd almost forgotten what Heather looked like when she played.

And still her heart would not stop aching.

Laney spotted Bill on a bench in the corner of the quad at lunch. He sat between two of his friends, bent over an artist's sketchbook, oblivious of the noise around them.

As Laney walked up, she heard Bill say, "I think I've finally found what I really love. It's the coolest thing. They just come to me in my dreams."

She looked down at the sketchbook on Bill's knees and felt the blood drain from her face. Bill had drawn a perfect portrait of Pinchpenny, but his clothes were fresh and dapper, instead of the worn cast-offs Laney knew he wore.

"Oh hey, Laney. What's up?" The apathy in Bill's voice slapped her in the face.

"I... I..." she stammered. "I just hadn't seen you in a while and was wondering if we could hang out sometime?"

"Oh. Um... I don't know how to say this, Laney, but you're just not my type," he said. The boys on either side of him snickered into their hands.

"But... what about..." She searched Bill's face for an emotion, any emotion but only saw polite indifference in his eyes. "Never mind."

Laney backed away, holding her books tight to her chest. She turned quickly so they wouldn't see the tears threatening to spill down her cheeks. A cloud passed over the sun, and Laney wondered if her heart would ever stop aching.

# Charm City

Lisbeth mounted the stairs to the row house apartment she shared with her grandmother in the Highlandtown neighborhood. Her legs protested as she rounded up the third flight of stairs. She'd already had a long night on her feet at the coffee house, but the tiny, third-floor apartment, with no elevator, was what she and her grandmother could afford between Social Security and tips.

The front door creaked as she slipped inside, and Lisbeth hoped it wasn't enough to wake her grandmother. She paused and listened for a moment and didn't hear anything, so she thought she was home free. Lisbeth set about washing her apron in the kitchen sink, trying to get out the pastry flour, whipped cream, and general schmutz before her next shift tomorrow. Leaving it to soak, she watered the small, potted herbs in the window just above the sink.

"Elisabetta?" called a thin voice from the back room.

Lisbeth felt her shoulders droop. Being as sick as she was, Lisbeth's grandmother needed all the sleep she could get, and she felt guilty for waking her.

Lisbeth wiped her wet hands on her pants as she peeked around the door into her grandmother's dim bedroom. "Yes, Yaya?"

"Elisabetta? Where are you?" Yaya's voice was becoming querulous, and she patted the bed on either side of her. Her eyesight was not good on the best of days, and in the shadow-filled bedroom, she was all but blind.

"I'm here, Yaya," Lisbeth said as edged next to the bed and took her grandmother's hand, patting it. "What do you need?"

"I need you, child. It's time," she said, grasping Lisbeth's hand tight.

"Time for what, Yaya? Do you need to go to the bathroom?"

"No, it's time for me to go, silly girl." Lisbeth's grandmother rolled to her side so she could grab Lisbeth's left hand in both of hers.

"Go where? It's the middle of the night. You're not making much sense, Yaya."

"I'm about to die, and I need to pass on my knowledge, you daft child!" Yaya grunted as she twisted Lisbeth's hand around so that it was palm up. Lisbeth gasped and started to squawk a protest. But Yaya had other ideas.

Lisbeth's grandmother stabbed the sharp fingernail of her index finger into the center of her granddaughter's palm and twisted. Lisbeth yelped and tried to pull away, but her grandmother held her fast. The skin tore and blood welled up.

"Agape," intoned Lisbeth's grandmother, and she stabbed her finger down and twisted again.

"Yaya, stop! You're hurting me!" shouted Lisbeth.

"Alhim," she said, followed by a grunt as she had to hold tight to Lisbeth, who was trying to pull away. She missed at first, but then she steadied Lisbeth's hand enough to stab her finger down into the bloody and tender palm a third time.

"Yaya, please!" Lisbeth was starting to sob.

"Thelema," she pronounced and struggled to hold her granddaughter's wrist tight. Both women were grunting and struggling.

As Lisbeth's grandmother started to win the battle and steady her granddaughter's hand again, she spat into Lisbeth's abused palm and said, "Jahbulon!" The she slapped her own palm against Lisbeth's and twisted hard. "Lux!" she cried.

Lisbeth felt dizzy, and her knees shook like water. She fell to the floor, and her grandmother finally released her wrist. When she woke ten minutes later, her grandmother was dead. Before Lisbeth called Witzky's Funeral Home, she cleaned the blood from her grandmother's hand and bandaged her own palm as she cried. She couldn't stand the thought of some stranger knowing about her grandmother's bizarre moment of insanity at the end.

By the time Lisbeth went back to work, her palm had healed, leaving a strange, swirling scar in the center. Her first day back seemed to pass in a fog. Her body knew all the motions, and her mouth said all the right things, but she felt like she was watching from the outside. For the first time since she'd moved to Baltimore and started to work at a local coffee house so that she could take care of Yaya, her grandmother wouldn't be there when Lisbeth got home. Yaya was miles away out on German Hill Road, buried in the family plot in the Polish Catholic cemetery.

Lisbeth finished her shift and thanked everyone for their kindness, the casseroles they'd sent while she was out, and the hugs they'd given her when she came back. She walked home up Thames Street toward her empty apartment and pondered getting a cat for company, if nothing else. She didn't even notice the short, dumpy man with dishwater-blond hair and a bad tan suit rushing past her, consulting the printed directions in his hand. Lisbeth's left palm itched as he passed, and she thought that a short-haired cat would be less trouble than a long-haired cat.

The man was waiting for Lisbeth when she got into work the next day. He fiddled with his silverware, and his glasses, and his napkin, and looked everywhere but at Lisbeth when she came to take his order. Lisbeth thought he was strange but just weird-strange not dangerous-strange, so she plastered on a smile and hoped that she could add good tipper to her mental description of the frumpy little man.

"Hi there," she chirped. "What can I get you?"

"Black coffee," he muttered down into the table.

Lisbeth waited a moment to see if he'd add a pastry or sandwich, but the man kept his eyes glued to the table in front of him. She shrugged and brought him a generous mug of black coffee.

Setting the cup on the table without a clatter, she said, "Here you go," still trying to be perky and hold out hope for a good tip. As she was withdrawing her hand, the man's hand shot forward, and he bumped the inside of her wrist with his fingertips. There was hardly any force to it at all, but Lisbeth jerked her hand back anyway but not before she flexed open her palm.

The man saw the swirling scar there. "It is you," he gasped and looked up at Lisbeth for the first time. He poked his glasses back up the bridge of his nose and smiled. "I'd like a love charm, please."

"Okay," Lisbeth said as she backed away from the table. "Let me go check on that in the back."

Her manager escorted the confused man out moments later and invited him to never return. Lisbeth watched from the safety of the back of the shop and bit her lip. The man had been creepy and strange, but she couldn't shake the vision that came into her head the moment he'd said love charm - the vision of dried rose petals, lilac blooms, and a piece of budding willow branch sewn up in red satin with pink and white thread and the sound of the exact words to say as she did it, even though the words seemed like nonsense to her.

Lisbeth's nerves had calmed by the time the strange Eastern European gentleman showed up a few weeks later. He was tall with swooping dark hair, a thick mustache, and just enough of a hint of his homeland in his voice to sound a little exotic but still fully American. He always asked for Lisbeth, and he always had coffee and a croissant as he read the newspaper, no matter what time of the day or night it was, and he always paid cash. When Lisbeth was not on shift, the other servers reported to her that he would smile and say, "no, thank you" to sitting with another server and leave without a backward glance with his newspaper tucked under his arm. They were all bitterly disappointed because he was a lavish tipper. Lisbeth wondered sometimes if the man was someone she should be worrying about, but the money was good, and he was no trouble at all to take care of.

Then, on a slow and ordinary Thursday afternoon about two months after he first started frequenting the coffee house, the man finally said something to Lisbeth besides his order and thank you. The café was empty except for him, Lisbeth, and a local writer buried in her laptop in the corner.

"I'm sorry," he said. "I hope I'm not being any trouble, but your last name... it wouldn't be Dabrowski, would it? I'm sorry... I shouldn't ask." He shook his head.

"Um, actually, yes, my last name is Dabrowski," said Lisbeth. "Why do you ask? I hope I'm not in some kind of trouble." She forced a little laugh.

"Oh, no, Miss. It's just that you look so much like someone my father once knew." The man flashed brilliantly white teeth. "Is there anyone in your family named Agatha?"

"Yes." Lisbeth drew the word out and wished her manager hadn't stepped out to the bank to get change. "Why?"

"I know this seems odd," the man began, and he leaned forward with his elbows on the table. Lisbeth took a step back. "But my father, he loved this woman named Agatha when he was a young man back in

Poland. She was quite the beauty... so vivacious and alive. Father hoped to marry her, but Agatha fell in love with another man, a man named Dabrowski, and she married him and moved to America."

Lisbeth's eyes went wide, and she put her hand to her mouth.

"This means something to you, yes?" The man looked at her, and Lisbeth nodded without saying a word. He smiled at her again. "I thought it might, because, you see, my father has this picture of his beautiful Agatha that he took of her when they went on a picnic. He never stopped loving her, and you... you look just like her. You have her cheekbones and her eyes, but she kept her hair long, and yours is short."

"Yaya always liked to keep her hair long. She was always trying to get me to grow mine out." Lisbeth's voice was soft and small as fingers wandered up to touch her short bob.

"Agatha is your grandmother? That's wonderful! Maybe we can do something good, you and I. Maybe we can bring the old lovebirds back together."

"I'm sorry, Mr..." Lisbeth paused.

"Call me Tomasz! Surnames are so formal."

Lisbeth cleared her throat and tried to blink her tears away. "I'm sorry, Tomasz, but my Yaya passed away a few months ago, last April."

"Oh! Oh, I am so sorry to bring up such fresh grief," Tomasz reached for her hand and squeezed it, and Lisbeth let him. "Here." He handed her a real linen handkerchief. "Please sit down." He gestured to the chair across from him.

Lisbeth slipped into the seat and dabbed her eyes and blew her nose. She was grateful for the chance to sit before her rebellious knees gave way.

"I am so sorry for your loss," said Tomasz, gripping his hands together in front of him on the table. "My father, he will be devastated. I think he always hoped that he would see his lovely Agatha again and that this time maybe he could win her heart."

Lisbeth managed to produce a wan smile. "I'm sorry for your father. I never knew about the romance. Yaya didn't like to talk about the old country. She said it was better to look forward instead of looking back."

Tomasz bellowed a deep belly laugh and slapped his knee. "That sounds just like the Agatha my father described to me: always look forward, never back."

Lisbeth nodded and fidgeted with the edge of her apron. Silence stretched between the two.

"I should get back to work before my manager gets back," she said. "He doesn't like to see us sitting down on the job, even if it is slow."

"Yes, yes," said Tomasz. "I would not want to get you in trouble. Thank you for your time."

Lisbeth went behind the counter to fetch the coffee pot to pour each of her customers a warm up, but by the time she turned around, Tomasz was gone.

A week later, in the middle of a thunderstorm in the early afternoon, Tomasz came back to the coffee house. It was much busier than the last time he and Lisbeth had talked, with a more than a dozen locals and tourists crowded inside the small shop waiting for the storm to pass. Lisbeth saw Tomasz from across the room and waved to one of the few empty seats in the house. He'd just finished settling down and pulling his newspaper out of its plastic sleeve when she arrived with his usual.

"Such a wonderful lady." He flashed his brilliant smile again. "You always remember."

Lisbeth laughed. "Is there anything else you need, Tomasz?"

"I have everything I need for now," he said. "But I was wondering what time your shift is over."

"Oh, I..." Lisbeth blushed.

"Oh, no! No, I'm not asking you on a date. Not that you aren't a lovely young woman." It was the first time Lisbeth had ever seen Tomasz flustered. "I was just wondering because I have something for you from my father, and I'd like to talk to you a little more about your grandmother."

"Oh, well, that's fine then." Lisbeth laughed again. "It all depends on how long we stay busy, but I should be off between three and four."

"Until then." Tomasz saluted her with a smile and his coffee cup.

It stayed busy until there was a break in the rain, and then most of the patrons made a run for wherever else they had to be. By the time Lisbeth was done counting out and settling all her checks at nearly five o'clock, the rain had started up again. This time it seemed angrier, with more wind and cracks of thunder and lightning.

Lisbeth settled down across the table from Tomasz with her own mug of coffee in her hands. She let out an appreciative sigh as she stretched her legs out in front of her and wiggled her toes in her shoes.

"Ah, good!" said Tomasz. "I was starting to think I might have to read the more pedestrian parts of the paper, like the sports section." He leaned in with a conspiratorial whisper.

"Well," said Lisbeth as the corner of her mouth quirked up. "I'm glad I could save you from the horror of earned run averages."

"You are a very good woman." Tomasz nodded and winked.

Setting her coffee on the table and leaning forward, Lisbeth said, "So, what's this thing you have for me from your father? I've been dying of curiosity."

Tomasz smiled and reached into his jacket pocket. He pulled a small brown leather jewelry box and laid it on the table between them. Lisbeth kept her hands clasped between her knees and leaned forward. Tomasz crossed his arms leaning back with a smirk.

"What is it?" she breathed.

"Why don't you open it and find out?" Tomasz chuckled.

"Really?" Lisbeth looked up at Tomasz with her eyes wide. He gestured to the box impatiently.

Lisbeth reached out with trembling fingers and gently pried the lid up. Laid on yellowing velvet was a thick, oval silver locket, decorated from top to bottom in delicate scroll work and floral flourishes. The thick rope chain wrapped around the edge of the locket in a neat spiral. "It's beautiful," Lisbeth gasped.

"My father was going to give it to your grandmother when he asked her to marry him. He thought it would be much more practical than a ring, since she would be a farmer's wife. Once they had children, she could put their photos in there in keep them close to her heart always. Father saved for almost a year, working an extra job to make the money. He hardly ever saw Agatha, but he felt sure she loved him just as much as he loved her and she knew what he was doing. When the day finally came, he went to her father's house and found that she'd eloped with Dabrowski and moved to America the week before." Tomasz sighed.

"Oh, Tomasz, I am so sorry. That must have broken his heart," Lisbeth said.

"It did," Tomasz said. "My father did eventually go on to get married and have children - obviously, since I am here - but I think Agatha was always his true love, and he never got over her."

Lisbeth and Tomasz stared at the locket on the table between them, each lost in thought.

Tomasz broke the silence. "You should try it on."

"What?" Lisbeth startled up into a straight backed position. "No. I couldn't. It belongs to your father."

"But it should have been your grandmother's, and since she's not here anymore, who better to have it?" Tomasz gestured to her with his palms up. Lisbeth bit her lip and twisted her fingers in her lap. Tomasz scooped the locket up and dangled it from the tips of his fingers, letting the sparkling oval swing and twirl in front of Lisbeth's eyes. "It's supposed to be yours."

Lisbeth licked her lips and said, "But I can't. It's obviously very expensive. You could probably sell it for a lot of money at an antiques store or one of those places that does estate jewelry."

"I don't care about the money," Tomasz said, holding out the locket closer to Lisbeth. "I just want to see the locket where it belongs... with you."

Lisbeth pinched her lips together, shaking her head. She started to speak, but Tomasz interrupted her.

"If it's about the value of it, how about a trade?"

Lisbeth let out a short, barking laugh. "What have I got to offer you? Coffee? I'll be serving you and anyone else you bring in here free coffee for the rest of my life."

"Heaven's sake, no!" Tomasz laid the locket against the velvet again, then clasped his hands in front of him. "This is going to sound silly, but did your grandmother still make those little old country charm bags? I don't believe in their power, of course, but if you still had one that your grandmother made it would make such a lovely memento for my father. We could trade!" Tomasz smiled wide, but Lisbeth drew back with her arms crossed across her chest, and her eyes narrowed.

"I have no idea what you're talking about," she mumbled and looked toward the door.

"Oh, no," said Tomasz, pressing his fingers to his mouth. "I have offended you. I am so sorry. It was just that my father spoke so fondly of these colorful little bags his Agatha made, and I thought if there might be one laying around the house that you and I might trade, then you wouldn't feel bad about the locket." Tomasz pushed the locket toward her. "Please, here, take it. It really should be yours."

Lisbeth's shoulders relaxed, and she let her hands drop into her lap. "I'm sorry, Tomasz, it's not you. There was a man who came in months ago looking for a love charm, and he was just so creepy that I want to stay as far away from that as possible."

"Ah, I understand." Tomasz looked down at the table and sighed. "Father will be disappointed, but I do understand."

Lisbeth squirmed in her chair. "It's just that there aren't any hanging around the house. Yaya didn't leave anything like that behind. I wish I could give you one to your father, but there just aren't any to give." Her words all came out in a rush.

"I understand, Lisbeth, I really do. Please, just take the locket. It's not like you could make any new ones that I could pass on to my father and just tell him that it was from Agatha's hands and give him some comfort in his final days." Tomasz's smile was small and wistful.

In Lisbeth's head, colors and herbs and plants and stitches and foreign words bounced and whispered, colorful packets with heady scents begging to be made. She almost wanted to shout to relieve the pressure. "I could make him one," she blurted. "What kind does he want?"

It was Tomasz's turn to gasp. "You would do that, for me? To bring comfort to a dying old man?"

Lisbeth nodded fiercely, this time clutching her fingers tight because they itched, and she had to keep them from twitching.

"Well," said Tomasz. "I really don't think my father would care what kind of charm it was, so long as he believed it to be from his Agatha. But I think it would be nice to have something that would bring him a little money, something for prosperity to make his life a little easier. I try to be a good son and do what I can, but these times are hard, you know?"

Lisbeth barely heard the last of what Tomasz said, her head was so filled with images and sounds - a whole nutmeg with a hole drilled through for her to draw through a piece of bright red thread together with little pieces of tiger's eye and sandalwood in a green cotton pouch stitched shut with gold thread, and the syllables of a foreign language ringing in her head.

"Hold on to the locket until I get the charm put together for you," Lisbeth said as she stood. "Would Tuesday be good for you?"

"Tuesday would be fine." He grabbed Lisbeth's hand as she headed for the door. "Maybe you could make one for me, too? I know I said I don't believe, but I am the low man at my office, and if it could help... perhaps you could make me something to attract power and make people think well of me?"

"Sure." Lisbeth's voice was soft and distracted as she pulled her hand from Tomasz's and headed for the door. She would need a piece of citrine the size of her thumb, clover and goldenseal to wrap around it, and just a pinch of ginger before she sewed the red satin shut with matching red thread.

When Lisbeth arrived for her shift on Tuesday, Tomasz was already there. He was pacing the sidewalk in front of the coffee house, checking his watch every 30 seconds. Lisbeth touched him on the shoulder and jumped back when he wheeled around, his face dark like thunder. He dropped his hands to his sides and unclenched his fists.

"Lisbeth," he said. "I am so sorry. I didn't mean to startle you. I'm just a little on edge. My father has taken a turn for the worse. I shouldn't be here; I really should be at the hospital. But I just thought if I could get the charm for him..." Tomasz ran this hand through his hair.

"Of course! I'm so sorry, Tomasz. I hope your father feels better." Lisbeth dug through her satchel for the vivid bundles and held them out. Tomasz snatched them from her hands and held them up to his nose, eyes nearly fluttering shut as he inhaled deeply.

"Thank you," he said as he began to turn away. "I'm sure Father will find great comfort in them."

"Tomasz?" Lisbeth called.

Tomasz turned with the charms clutched close to his chest, his voice tight and sharp. "What?"

"I don't mean to be a pain," Lisbeth said. "But the locket?"

"Oh, yes, yes." Tomasz fumbled in his pocket. "How silly of me. I can't keep a thought in my head since father got worse." He pulled out the familiar brown jewelry box and held it out to Lisbeth.

As Lisbeth took it, she said, "I could make your father a healing charm, too, if you think it would help?"

"No, no," Tomasz said as he backed away. "This will be fine. This is all I need."

Tomasz almost sprinted down the sidewalk as Lisbeth watched him go with a furrowed brow and a frown.

After that, Lisbeth relaxed a lot more about people seeking her out for charms. She thought the man in the bad tan suit seeking a love charm probably hadn't been that bad at all; she had just been unfamiliar with the way it all worked. People of all shapes and sizes began to show up at the coffee house looking for Lisbeth and for things that were off the menu. Most of them wanted charms for love or money, a few for healing, a small handful just wanted a plain good luck charm, and one woman wanted an special charm that combined igniting her husband's lust and keeping him faithful at the same time. Lisbeth developed a price list in her head, and before long, she was making more from the charms than she was from her tips.

Lisbeth almost lost her job at the coffee house because her boss thought she had started selling drugs. It seemed like an obvious assumption for all the small packets quickly changing hands for cash only. But he changed his tune after Lisbeth put together a successful business charm for him and nailed it over the door. Business tripled, and Lisbeth's boss said she could come and go as she pleased. She didn't even have to serve coffee if she didn't want to, as long as she "kept that good mojo going." Everything seemed to be going so well until a slender Asian woman with spikes of hot pink hair scattered in her short bob showed up asking for Lisbeth.

She came up to Lisbeth, who was wiping the front counter. "Hey, are you the one who has the charms?"

"That's me," Lisbeth said with a bright smile. "What kind are you looking for?"

The young woman smiled back and said, "It's for my brother, and he's a little bit shy about it. He's waiting out back."

"For your brother, right." Lisbeth nodded. She'd gotten used to some of her customers being ashamed of buying her wares. "I'm going out for a minute, Kevin," she called to her boss as she untied her apron and stashed it behind the counter. He waved her on without even a glance, focused as he was on making yet another pot of coffee for the steady stream of customers.

The two young women walked a few yards down the block in silence, then turned into the narrow alleyway. About halfway down its length, deep in the late afternoon shadows, Lisbeth turned to ask the young woman if they really were seeking out her brother or if being out of sight here would be fine for transacting their business. The young woman grabbed her by the shoulders and slammed Lisbeth up against the alley wall.

"Just what in the hell do you think you're doing? Huh?"

"What? Ow! I have no idea what you're talking about." Lisbeth tried to feint right, but the young woman just dug her fingers in deeper and pusher her harder up against the wall.

"Don't play dumb with me." The young woman's pretty face twisted up in a snarl.

"I'm not playing," Lisbeth whimpered. "I really have no idea what you're talking about. But I'll make you anything you want, free of charge, if you'll just stop hurting me."

The Asian woman's arms relaxed a little, and she narrowed her eyes. "You really don't know? Did Tommy not tell you anything?"

"Who's Tommy? Tell me what?"

"You don't know any Tommys? Don't lie to me," she growled and tightened her grip.

"I swear I don't know any Tommys," Lisbeth's voice trembled on the edge of hysteria. "The closest I know is a Tomasz. He used to be one of my coffee regulars, but he hasn't been around for a couple of months."

"Describe him to me."

Lisbeth described Tomasz to the Asian woman and kept right on babbling, telling her the whole story of how they had met, his father's current illness and romance with her grandmother back in the old country, and the locket and exchanging it for the charms.

"Oh, shit." The woman let Lisbeth go and stepped back. "He really did dupe you. I'm really sorry for cornering you like this, but we need to talk."

"Honestly, you make me kind of nervous. Why should I trust you after what you just did?" Lisbeth rubbed her shoulders.

"I get it, I do," the Asian woman said, holding her hands up palms out. "I'll stick to your rules, we can talk anywhere you want, but I really need to talk to you."

"At least tell me your name first," Lisbeth said.

"I'm Jenny." She held out her hand. Lisbeth hesitated for a moment, then she shook it.

Lisbeth and Jenny grabbed two cups of coffee to go at the coffee house and headed right back out. They found a bench on the Fell's Point dock and sat side by side, sipping coffee and watching the red neon of the Dominoe's Sugar sign over the harbor get brighter and brighter against the falling evening.

"First off," Jenny said. "His name is really Tommy, not Tomasz, and he's from Detroit, not Poland. And he's really done a number on you."

"But he gave me this locket that his father was going to use to propose to my grandmother." Lisbeth pulled the locket out from under her shirt to show Jenny.

Jenny looked close and snorted. "You can get something like that almost anywhere; those overdone, baroque styles are really popular right now. It doesn't even look like it's good sterling."

Lisbeth's face fell. "But..."

"How much do you know about your heritage?" Jenny interrupted her.

"I'm full Polish on my dad's side, but my mom is Polish and English mixed."

"No, no, no. How much do you know about your charms heritage?"

Lisbeth blushed. "Only what comes to me when people ask for charms. When somebody asks for something specific, it just pops into my head what to make and what to say while I'm doing it."

Jenny groaned and buried her face in one hand. "Damn it."

"What do you mean? What's going on? Would everybody stop being so damn mysterious and tell me what going on?" Lisbeth's voice was sharp.

"Lisbeth, you need to be quiet and listen to me. I'll tell you everything you want to know, but you have to listen and not interrupt. Understand?"

Lisbeth nodded.

"Okay," Jenny let out a deep breath. "Let's start out with that I'm a witch."

Lisbeth drew in her breath to speak, but Jenny held up her hand. "Remember about listening? And really? You're going to twitch over me being a witch when you stuff odds and ends in little bags, say a few words, and then they make things happen?"

"Point taken," Lisbeth mumbled into her coffee cup while she blushed and tried to avoid Jenny's gaze.

"Okay, so, we both do magical things but with different focuses. I'm a witch, and you're a charmer. Even though I can make charms and you can cast spells, neither one of us is nearly as strong as the other when it comes to our focuses because of where our natural talent lies. Got it?"

Lisbeth nodded and kept her lips pressed together.

"Good," Jenny continued. "The charming talent is always hereditary. You are part of a long line of charmers, very powerful charmers. Your grandmother was one of the three Kulinski sisters, but she lost her older sister in a threshing accident and her younger sister to rheumatic fever. It seems that when they died, their talent came to roost in your grandmother, and she became much more powerful. She refused to use her power for a long time, but after she married and came to America, she just couldn't seem to help it. She had to help other people. Dabrowski charms became legendary, the most powerful charms anyone had ever seen. Now, Agatha never had any daughters, so people in the magical community thought that was the end of Dabrowski charms. We're not sure why, but the charming talent only shows up in women. We have male witches and female witches but never any male charmers. But it looks like charming talent can skip a generation because here you are." Jenny gestured to Lisbeth.

Lisbeth raised her eyebrows. "But that still doesn't explain why you tried to beat me up in an alley and why you think Tomasz, or Tommy, whatever, pulled some kind of con on me."

"Your charms have been going bad, Lisbeth, real bad, all except for the ones you made for Tommy."

"What do you mean they've been going bad? The ones I made for the coffee house have been working just fine." Lisbeth said. "And you just said I'm some sort of a super duper kind of charmer."

"Your charms are just as powerful as your grandmother's ever were, but they seem to be going bent. The results keep twisting. Like your love charms, most of them seem to be resulting in stalkers instead of lovers," said Jenny.

"I must be doing something wrong," said Lisbeth. "But I do just what I see in my head, and that's what I did for the coffee house and for Tomasz."

Jenny squinched up her nose and thought. "Wait a minute, back in the alley you said you would make me whatever I wanted, free of charge. You haven't been taking money for your charms, have you?"

"Well, yeah," Lisbeth said. "What else am I supposed to do, give them away? I've got bills to pay, and if that's my talent..."

Jenny pinched the bridge of her nose and sighed. "You can't trade magic for money, Lisbeth. It sours the magic. You can give it away, and you can barter, but you can never, ever take money for it."

"How am I supposed to know that?" Lisbeth threw her hands up in the air. "Is there some instruction manual I never got?"

"No," Jenny said. "Your grandmother was supposed to teach you how to handle your power responsibly, just like her mother taught her. And since she's passed beyond the veil, there's no sure way to find out why she didn't do her duty." Jenny frowned.

"Hey." Lisbeth straightened up. "No ragging on my Yaya."

"Sorry." Jenny gave an apologetic half smile. "You're right, I shouldn't speak ill of the dead. It's just that I'm frustrated. My fellow witches and I have been chasing your bad charms all over town trying to minimize the damage, and meanwhile, Tommy is using all his new found money and power to make trouble for us."

"What's wrong with Tommy, anyway? Why is being such a jerk?"

Jenny shrugged. "No idea. He blew into town a few years ago, and up until now, all of his schemes have been small time. But now with Dabrowski charms to back him up, he's become more than just a petty crook. If he keeps up the way he's going, he'll have all the black magic in town under his control...then who knows what he'll do." Jenny shuddered.

"This is all my fault." Lisbeth sagged forward with her elbows on her knees, then she took a deep breath and looked up at Jenny. "What can I do to help? I mean, I have to help fix this."

Jenny nodded. "First thing, stop selling charms for money. It's fine to use it as a means of support, but barter the charms for things you need, like food or new furniture."

Lisbeth nodded furiously. "And?"

"You need to help us stop Tommy. We can dispell any of the charms that went wrong, but since his are working just fine, you're the only one who can pull them apart. Well, he could pull them apart, too, but I sincerely doubt he will."

"So how do we do that?"

"Tommy's attending a charity event on Saturday night to schmooze the powerful mundanes of the city. He always keeps the charms on him. Are you up for a little pick-pocketing?" Jenny raised her eyebrows.

"I'm in." Lisbeth's mouth tightened into a thin line.

Lisbeth wore her best dress: a sleeveless, floor-length black velvet number that showed plenty of cleavage. It was the only thing she had that was nice enough to wear to a black tie charity event, and she hoped it wasn't too far out of style given that she'd bought it ten years ago for her freshman formal.

Jenny snuck her in the back way, courtesy of a witch from her coven who made her living as a banquet server. Lisbeth peered out from behind the polyester curtains that hid the service area from the view of the guests. She fiddled with her locket and shifted from foot to foot.

"Do you see him?" Jenny whispered in her ear.

"Not yet," Lisbeth whispered back, not taking her eyes from the milling crowd. "It's hard to tell the difference when they're all wearing penguin suits."

"Well, go take a closer look." Jenny shoved Lisbeth from the safety of the curtain. Lisbeth stumbled and started to turn back, but Jenny made shooing motions and hissed at her to get going. Glancing around herself, Lisbeth hoped no one had noticed her clumsy entrance, but no one gave her a second look.

Lisbeth started to wander around, wondering how she was going to find one man in this huge ballroom full of people. She turned down a glass of champagne from a passing waiter and sighed. She had no idea where to start.

"You really should have taken the glass," said a familiar voice behind her. Lisbeth startled around and placed her hand on her chest. There was Tomasz/Tommy looking suave and debonair in his tuxedo, cradling a martini in his hand. "I can call him back over if you want me to." He spoke without a trace of the accent he'd used while coming to the coffee house.

Lisbeth's mouth worked up and down, like a fish out of water, and her brain raced, trying to think of what to say to get the charms from him.

"Or maybe we should get a glass for Jenny. I'm sure she's very thirsty." Tommy smiled and sipped his drink.

"How did you..."

"How did I know Jenny got to you?" Tommy laughed. "Pretty simple, really. I knew she'd eventually make contact, and I had to get what I needed from you before she did. She was probably waiting for you to finish grieving for your dear, departed Yaya, but it worked out better for me for you to still be grieving."

"You bastard." Lisbeth balled up her fists at her sides. "You used me."

Tommy mock gasped. "Such language. You wound me!" Then he tossed back his head and roared laughter. "It's use or be used, honey. You should have learned that by now." He drained his martini glass and motioned to a waiter for another.

"So everything you said to me was a lie? There wasn't one bit of truth to it?" Lisbeth hugged herself.

Tommy made a show of thinking for a long minute. "I think I called you pretty once, and that's not a lie. You really should use that to your advantage, you know." He winked.

Lisbeth let her arms drop and smiled a fluttery smile, "Maybe you could teach me some of your tricks," she said, looking at him up through her eyelashes and stepping a little closer.

"Oh no, honey," he said as he took a giant step back. "You're going to have to be a lot less obvious if you want to fool me."

"But..." she began and took another step closer.

Tommy stepped back again, right into the waitress who had let Lisbeth and Jenny in the back door. Canapés scattered everywhere, and boursin cheese smeared all over Tommy's tuxedo. The tray was still clattering on the floor as she apologized.

"I am so sorry, sir," she said as she whipped out a large linen serving napkin from the back of her belt and tried to wipe the mess from Tommy's jacket. "I'm sure my company will pay for the cleaning bill." She kept wiping, and Tommy tried to push her hands away.

"It's fine, it's fine," he growled. "I was ready to go home anyway." He finally pushed her off. The crowd was gawking.

Eyes narrowed, he stared at Lisbeth as he strode toward the exit. He passed close to her, not close enough to touch but close enough to hear.

"Stay away from me, you bitch," he hissed. "Or I will make you very sorry. You have no idea what I can do."

Lisbeth drew back as if he'd slapped her and ran for the service area in tears. Jenny was waiting for her.

"How did it go?" Jenny asked as Lisbeth snatched up another linen serving napkin and dabbed at her eyes.

"Okay, I think," she said. "I think he bought it."

They both turned toward the polyester curtain and held their breaths until it twitched a moment later. It was the serving witch, and she held up the two charms with a triumphant grin.

"Carrie, you're brilliant!" Jenny crowed as she caught up her friend in a tight hug.

"Sometimes spending the summer in Romania with the less desirable element pays off." Carrie laughed, then turned to Lisbeth and held out the charms. "I think there's something you wanted to do with these."

Lisbeth pressed her lips together and gathered the charms close to her chest.

"Why don't we go where we can get a little privacy?" Jenny suggested, and the ladies retreated from the kitchen.

Out behind the hotel, in a narrow alley under the waning moonlight, Lisbeth looked to Jenny for advice.

"What do I do?" she said. "Nothing is coming to me."

"I'm not surprised," Jenny said. "It's not natural to destroy your own work." She sighed. "What you need to do is pull it apart and scatter the components. It's not difficult, but it is hard."

"How hard could it be?" Lisbeth shrugged and started to pull the seams of the money charm apart. Pain ripped through her abdomen and sent her gasping to her knees. Jenny went to her and held her shoulders while she shuddered.

"Why didn't you warn me?" Her voice was hoarse and thin.

"Could anything I said have prepared you for this?" Jenny looked to Lisbeth, who shook her head. "Because you put so much of yourself into the charms, it's going to hurt when you destroy them. I'm so sorry, Lisbeth, but it can't be helped."

Lisbeth nodded and quickly ripped into the bag again, and her face grew paler. She picked the red thread out of the nutmeg with shaking fingers, snapped the piece of sandalwood in two, and cast the bits of tiger's eye into the alleyway muck.

"Will the next one be just as bad?" Her voice quivered.

"Probably worse, since it's a power charm," said Jenny, and she hugged Lisbeth hard.

Lisbeth sobbed and felt a tear slide down her cheek. "I better do it now, or I don't think I'll ever be able to do it." Lisbeth held the power charm in both her hands and blew out a breath.

She tore it fast, like ripping off a band-aid, and cried out in pain. From the open mouth of the alley came an answering roar of rage. It was Tommy in his stained tux with his hair all disheveled.

"You bitch!" he shouted and started running down the alley to where Lisbeth and Jenny knelt on the ground.

Lisbeth's hands shook, but she tore the threads of goldenseal and clover into shreds and released them into the night wind. She shook out the red cloth, and the ginger sifted down and the chunk of citrine plopped into the mud. Jenny jumped up and interposed herself between Lisbeth and Tommy.

"Back-off, asshole," she growled. "She's one of ours now. If you hurt her, we'll hurt you back."

"Don't you know who I am?" He sneered.

"You're a two-bit hustler, Tommy. You don't have the charms anymore, so you're just back to being a two-bit hustler. Don't piss me off, or I'll toast your ass."

Tommy looked at the determination on Jenny's face and swallowed hard. He started to back away with his hands held up, palms out.

"I'm not going to forget about tonight," he said.

"Good," said Jenny. "Because neither will I."

She waited until Tommy was out of the alley before she turned to help Lisbeth to her feet.

"Let's get you home," she said. "I'm thinking you could probably do with a hot bath and a glass of wine right about now."

Lisbeth padded into her new living room and watched as her handyman finished hanging her new roman shades. True to her promise to Jenny, she'd stopped selling her charms for money, but she found that she could get quite a bit when she bartered. Her sunny, first-floor walk-up was courtesy of providing her new landlord with charms for peace and safety in all six of his buildings in the city. As long as the charms kept working, she could stay free of charge. The handyman hanging her shades was doing the work for a love charm he'd used when he proposed to his long-time girlfriend.

"Well," he said as he stepped back. "That should do it, Ms. Dabrowski. Just let me know if there's anything else I can do for you."

Lisbeth smiled and shook his hand. "Well, you just let me know if you need any other charms. I'm sure we can work something out."

He laughed and shook his head. "Ms. Dabrowski, you gave me my Katie. You still have plenty of credit with me."

Lisbeth shook her own head. "I don't know how much I had to do with it. She loves you; I'm sure she would have said yes."

"Sure, just like the last six times I asked her. You just call me if you need anything, okay?"

Lisbeth locked the door behind him and looked around at the beginning of her new life and smiled. Everything just might be okay.

# Stealing Uncle Louie

Heat radiated from the pavement and through the soles of his shoes, but Kevin kept up his carefully constructed, slouching stroll through the neighborhood. With a ball cap riding low over his eyes, a backpack slung over his right shoulder, and one hand tucked in his jeans pocket, he looked like any other hometown baseball fan making an early exit from a disappointing game to try to beat the traffic. The stadium reared up behind him, throwing bright light and the dull roar of the crowd into the twilight sky. The football stadium quietly crouched beside it, adding its own soft purple neon glow, but the football fans wouldn't emerge until it was much cooler.

Kevin had no idea whether or not today's game was going well, but he knew this was the sweet spot to leave if you wanted to look innocent without a lot of witnesses. Every part of his outfit, every move he made, was designed to make him look like the innocent everyman. Walking through the neighborhood to get to free street parking rather than pay the high prices at the stadium lots seemed reasonable, and the backpack for his own bottles of water and sandwiches to avoid paying the outrageous prices for ballpark refreshments just made him look like a thrifty fan. No one would think to look at him twice, and that was just the way Kevin liked it.

But even if this neighborhood wasn't interested in him, he was interested in it. Well appointed brick townhomes lined the street, nearly identical to each other except for a few small touches: geraniums in window boxes on one, a deep green door instead of the standard burgundy or brown on another. Even in their differences the houses were predictable, just like their owners. The corner of Kevin's mouth quirked up a hair. He'd taken this evening stroll enough times to know the rhythms of this neighborhood. He knew when they walked their dogs, visited their neighborhood bars, and had standing plans for dinner with friends; and he knew how long they'd be. A quick survey up and down the street showed that he was alone, as expected, and Kevin slipped down the alley to his right and jogged behind the houses. Third to the left was where he wanted to start. This couple was visiting her mother at an old folk's home in the north part of the county, just like they did every third Thursday. It was amazing what people would talk about in voices loud enough to hear when they were in their own little personal bubbles, getting into their cars and going on about their business.

Kevin also knew that their backdoor was practically wide open. They only locked the screen door, not the steel main door the builders had installed to discourage thieves. A few quick steps up and he was on their back porch. A look to the left and right and he was still alone, then he slipped on the heavy black leather gloves from his backpack and pulled out the box cutter. Two quick slits in the screen and he shoved his hand through and unlocked the screen door from the inside. He went through the back door like he owned the place. Kevin sneered. Rich people could be so dumb. He knew these houses were way out of reach for anyone from his working-class neighborhood, but one would think that the rich people would be better about protecting what they had. After all, that working-class neighborhood, full of poor people, both honest and not, looking for a way out, was just three streets over.

"Money don't buy brains," Kevin muttered and got to work.

He went through the drawers in the kitchen, methodically opening and closing each one until he found what he wanted.

"Bingo," he said, finding five crisp twenties tucked under the silverware tray, probably lunch money for the wife. People thought they were so clever, leaving home any cash they didn't need right away just in case of a mugging. Kevin grinned as he shoved the cash into his pocket.

He glided through the house looking for small things that were easy to pawn. If it looked rarely used, it was a bonus. It would take longer to report it stolen, if they ever did at all. In the husband's office, he scooped up an old mp3 player out of a drawer. Odds were the husband would just think it got lost in a move. The same drawer had an old hand-held gaming system, and that got dumped in the backpack, too. But most of the stuff in the office was too large or noticeable. He moved on to the bedroom.

He glanced in the bathroom first and noticed the jewelry scattered across one side of the counter. That would be the stuff the wife wore in a regular rotation, and he knew to leave it the hell alone. The jewelry box on her dresser, however, was a completely different story. It would most likely be her best stuff, which she didn't wear often. He slid open the little satin-lined drawers, and his grin got even bigger. A string of pearls and matching earrings, a diamond tennis bracelet, and a square-cut emerald ring all slid into the front pocket of his backpack. He left the old cameo behind. It was definitely worth some bucks, but it was too unique, too traceable.

Kevin doubled back to the bathroom and flipped open the medicine cabinet. The husband had a bad back, and the wife had anxiety issues, so it was a bonanza - Vicodin, Xanax, Valium, and even some Viagra. He knew the couple would notice right away, but the street value of the pills was just too good to pass up. He dropped the bottles into his bag and hoped they'd blame their housekeeper.

Kevin headed back down the stairs and breezed through the living room past the massive 52-inch flat screen hooked up to all the latest in home theater technology. Sure, it would fetch a good price at the pawn shop, but it would be awfully conspicuous to tote down the street. If he needed to, he could ditch the bag on his back in an alley or a dumpster, and there was nothing in the bag to tie it to him. This was why Kevin had a rap sheet only half as long as guys who pulled in the same kind of cash he did.

He locked the screen door on the way out and smoothed the ragged edges of the cut screen down, anything to delay the phone call to the cops and give the neighbors that much more time to forget about the baseball fan with the backpack they saw strolling down the street.

The next hit was two doors down, a young woman who lived alone and worked a lot of late nights and weekends. She actually locked her back door, but she'd never bothered to upgrade to a better deadbolt from the builder grade, and Kevin made short work of it with his lock picks. He walked into the kitchen and almost stepped on her cat, who hissed and ran. Taking a deep breath to calm his nerves, he then got down to work.

This lady's hidden cash stash in the kitchen was in a little ceramic Santa jar on top of her microwave, and it was only ten bucks. He shoved the ten into his pocket along with the twenties and shrugged. Money was money. Kevin prowled through the semi-darkened house with a frown on his face. There were no obvious shows of wealth here. The furniture was all cheap thrift store finds, durable but ugly, and all the electronics were from the last century. But there were books everywhere: in stacks on the coffee table, piled two deep on bookshelves, and in baskets next to the couch and recliner. Maybe upstairs would be more profitable.

Upstairs was just as bad. Two of the three bedrooms were empty, curtainless windows gaping and letting in the bright, harsh light from the streetlight outside. The one obviously occupied bedroom was decorated with the same thrift store aesthetic, dinged and dented bureaus, mismatched lamps, and books everywhere. Even the medicine cabinet was a disappointment; there was nothing stronger than aspirin.

"Sheesh," Kevin said under his breath. "This is a total bust."

He turned to go when a glimmer caught his eye. Hanging off the finial of a colonial blue ginger jar lamp gleaming against the dusty lampshade was a canary yellow diamond pendant. The huge, square gem drew Kevin across the room with his mouth agape.

"What are you doing in this shit hole?" he murmured, reaching for it before he even thought about it. He held it up to the streetlight streaming in the window, dangling from its chain, admiring the sparkle. It was at least a carat and a half, and he knew down to his toes that the owner would notice it missing immediately and call the cops. But if he could get it to his fence fast enough, he could get the pendant out of his hands and walk away with cash before the report went out. The diamond seemed to spin and twirl all on its own, daring him to take it. Kevin grinned and shoved it in his pocket instead of the bag. He headed back downstairs whistling a happy tune. His hand was on the back door when he heard the key in the front, and his stomach dropped, his mouth went dry. She was home early for once in her miserable life.

Kevin slid out the back and shut the door softly. He leapt off her back porch and sprinted for the nearest cross-street. He emerged out into early evening pedestrian traffic and immediately slowed to a fast walk. No sense attracting attention, but he would to have to hustle if he was going to get the diamond unloaded without getting caught.

A few lefts and couple of rights deeper into the heart of the city, away from the wide-eyed tourists and he was headed down the street to his favorite pawn broker with a spring in his step. Kevin looked left and looked right, then skipped across the street in the middle of the block. Another half-block up and he was home free. That was when the first car alarm went off - first the Buick, then the Dodge, then the raggedy old Cadillac, each as he passed them. Kevin knew that most of the car owners wouldn't bother with alarms; the cars were hunks of junk anyway. Yet there they all were, honking and squealing. Sweat popped out on Kevin's forehead. Heads all up and down the block were starting to turn.

Kevin reversed direction. There was another broker he could visit. His heart hammered hard against his chest as a city cruiser came around the corner and made a slow mosey up the block. The cop's eyes were everywhere, searching for the mischief-maker in charge of all the noise. When his eyes slid past Kevin without stopping, he let out the breath he was holding and headed east. He could have sworn he heard someone laughing over the receding sound of the car alarms, but he was alone.

Kevin's second favorite broker was happy to take the diamond, the other jewelry, and the old electronics off his hands. Fifteen minutes of banter and haggling, and he was back out on the street with a wad of cash in his pocket and headed out to find someone who would be interested in the pills. The same city cruiser that he'd passed to get away from the freaky car alarms was headed down the street straight for him. Kevin tried to play it cool and keep up his slouching gait like there was nothing to worry about with the law.

His shoulders loosened a bit when the cop car eased past him without stopping. But that didn't last long. Kevin saw the blue and red lights reflect on the white painted doorframe of the row house just ahead. A quick glance behind him confirmed that the cruiser was making a U-turn and had his lights on. Kevin ran.

He zigged into the first alley that presented itself and heard a single whoop of the car's siren behind him. Kevin didn't stop. He saw a dumpster up ahead and with only the merest hesitation, he chucked the backpack, and all the expensive pills, into the trash. He didn't waste any breath on cursing out loud, but in his head, he would have made the saltiest sailor proud. Those pills were worth a lot, and now they were going to make some bum rich. Kevin zagged into a cross alley to his left and heard another siren whoop behind him, sounding louder for bouncing off the walls of the alley.

Lengthening his stride and pouring on the speed, he nearly fell to the ground because of a stabbing pain in his right heel. He tried to ignore it, but the pain jabbed into his heel, shooting straight up his spine every time his right foot hit the pavement. Kevin hopped to a stop, trying not to put his right heel on the ground and looked behind him, panting. The blue and red lights reflected on the walls down at the mouth of the cross alley, but there were no cops running toward him. Maybe they were busy dumpster diving.

Kevin shrugged as he limped away to the nearest main road and tried to lose himself in the crowd. He hobbled along among the regular city dwellers out to walk their dogs, or get dinner, or get home from a late night at the office. Sweat rolled down his face and neck; each step was agony. His eyes ping-ponged from left to right, and he kept looking behind himself, expecting to see the city cruiser creeping up the street. But there was just the usual urban swirl of humanity, and none if it cared about him or who he was running from.

At an unoccupied bus stop bench, he wrenched off his shoe to find out what was causing him such torture. He expected a rock or a piece of asphalt, but when he peered into the shoe, Kevin saw the canary diamond pendant, all one and half carats of it, curled in the bottom of the heel. The heel of his sock was torn from the edges of the pendant, and he had gash in his flesh. Kevin fished out the pendant and held it up to the streetlight. Except for the smear of his blood, it looked just like it had when he'd pawned it less than an hour ago. Someone laughed behind him, and Kevin's head whipped around as he drew the diamond tight to his chest. There was no one there.

"Sonnava bitch," he muttered and looked all around again. No one was paying attention to him, and no one was laughing. Everyone was drawn into their own little bubbles and focused on their own agendas.

He worked his foot back into his sneaker, wincing. Wiping the streak of blood from the diamond with the hem of his t-shirt, he squinted up at the street signs above him. He needed to get rid of this diamond, and he needed to do it fast. In getting away from the cops, he had circled back and overshot his favorite pawn shop by a couple of blocks. He shoved the diamond in his pocket and got moving.

He looked around his trashed apartment full of early afternoon sunlight a few days later. There were beer bottles and half-smoked joints everywhere. One of his best friends was sprawled across the couch, drooling and snoring, and another was curled up on the kitchen floor under the table, asleep but twitching and whimpering. Kevin rubbed his eyes and ran his hand through his hair. It had been one hell of a party. Pawning the diamond twice had brought in enough money to clear up some debts with the neighborhood toughs and still keep him, his girl, and all his boys in booze, weed, and E for a couple of days straight.

Kevin started to look through all the assorted crap thrown around the living room, trying to find his jeans. He finally found them stuffed behind the old cast-iron radiator. Hoping there was still something left, he dug through the pockets. He found the five crisp twenties and crumpled ten, but that was it.

"Damn," he mumbled and stumbled back to his bedroom, yawning. Pulling his battered shades low to block out the afternoon sun, he was about to fall into bed when a sparkle caught his eye. There, laid out on the old milk crate that served as his night stand, was the canary diamond pendant, all one and half carats of it. He scooped it up and held it out, where it twirled and gleamed. It was the same pendant alright, but damned if he could remember how it got there. He thought he heard someone laughing, and he swallowed and hoped it was one the guys in the living room doing it in his sleep.

The shades jerked up all the way to the top of the window, flooding the room with bright light. The diamond seemed to explode with inner fire, throwing beautiful prisms all over the room. The clock radio on the milk crate came to life and started cruising through the stations until it found one playing Elvis, who was going on about being all shook up. Kevin gaped and didn't hear the front door open and close elsewhere in the apartment.

"Baby?" his girlfriend Cheryl called. "Are you here?" She walked into the bedroom, her high heels clicking on the bare wood floor. "There you are!" She snapped her gum and smiled.

Kevin turned to her with his mouth still open and still holding the pendant up in the air.

"Did I surprise you?" Then she saw the pendant and gasped. "Is that for me? Oh, please say that's for me."

"Uh, sure." He held out the pendant to her with a jerk of his arm.

Cheryl squealed and turned her back, then pulled up her peroxide-blonde hair to bare her neck. "Put it on me, put it on me!"

Kevin slid the pendant around her neck but his hands were shaking so badly that he had trouble doing up the clasp. He finally hooked it, and Cheryl scampered into the bathroom to check out her new pendant in the cracked mirror.

"Oh, honey, it's gorgeous!" And she darted back into the bedroom to wrap her arms around Kevin and cover his face with kisses.

"I'm glad you like it," he said in a bewildered voice.

"Oh, hey," Cheryl said drawing back a little. "I have some bad news, baby."

"What's that?"

"You know that pawn shop you usually deal with?"

"Yeah?" Kevin felt his belly tighten.

"Well, they got robbed this morning, and Al got roughed up bad. He says once he gets out of the hospital he's getting out of the business. He's going to move out to Montana and be with his kids. Weird, huh?"

He swallowed hard. "Yeah, weird."

"But there's other places you can go, right, baby?"

Kevin nodded dumbly.

Cheryl laughed and kissed Kevin on the lips. "Hey, baby?" she cooed. "I feel like showin' off my new jewelry tonight. Take me out someplace nice?" Kevin nodded again, and they used the cash he'd just found in his pocket to go to for the best crab cakes and rock fish the Inner Harbor could offer.

Kevin was hanging on the corner with his boys in the hot, sticky summer evening, smoking a cigarette, when Cheryl came down on him like a screaming hurricane.

"Where is it? Why'd you take it back?" She slapped her open palm against his chest.

"Take what, baby?" Kevin held his arms wide in confusion.

"My new necklace, you dick!" Cheryl screeched.

"I don't know what you're talkin' about. What are you bein' such a bitch for?" Kevin mumbled around his cigarette and threw his hands up in the air.

Cheryl crossed her arms over her chest. "I had it last night, and you spent the night, and now it's gone." She tapped the toe of her bright red stiletto on the pavement.

"And I'm the only one who could have taken it? Or you couldn't have lost it? Jesus, Cheryl, nice to know you trust me." Kevin shoved his hands into his pockets. His eyes widened as his right hand ran into something hard and square with a light chain.

"I'd probably trust you if you hadn't pulled this shit before."

Kevin shook his head and drove his hands deeper into to pockets to hide that they were shaking. "Forget this shit. I don't need to listen to you yell at me for something I didn't do. I'm outta here."

He threw his cigarette on the pavement and ground it out, then turned on his heel and stalked away. Behind him, he could hear Cheryl screaming at him to get back there this instant and calling him every foul name she could think of.

Half a block down and around a corner, he couldn't stand it anymore and pulled out whatever it was that had mysteriously appeared in his pocket. It was the canary yellow diamond pendant, all one and half carats of it. Kevin broke out into a cold sweat. He shoved the pendant back into his pocket and kept walking, trying to think as he went.

His feet just kept moving until he found himself in the flow of tourists wandering around the Inner Harbor. And that's when it struck him. Making his way to the edge of the water in a roundabout way, slowly and deliberately, he checked to make sure none of the foot patrol officers were looking. He dug the pendant out of his pocket, twirled it over his head like a cowboy twirls a lariat, and launched it out over the water. When he heard the plop as it hit the water the tightness around his heart eased. Several of the tourists walking by gave him strange looks, but Kevin just lit up a cigarette and made his way home with a smile on his face.

When Kevin got back to his place, something smelled odd, like dead fish and diesel fuel. He walked around the apartment sniffing and frowning, trying to find the source of the stink. It was in the bedroom. The canary diamond pendant lay in the middle of his bedroom floor in a puddle of dirty harbor water. Someone was laughing, even though he was alone.

Grabbing his head, he sank down to his knees. "Shit. Shit. Shit. Shit." His voice was soft and high pitched. The diamond just lay there and gleamed. Kevin finally grabbed the pendant and stuffed it in his pocket again and left the apartment.

He ran for a few blocks trying to think of what to do. Kevin pushed past people, not even hearing the squawks of protest. He stopped on a corner, turning in place, panting and looking for a place to ditch the diamond. People were staring at him and talking to each other behind their hands. In the distance, he heard a siren. Grabbing the diamond out of his pocket, he chucked it down the storm drain at his feet, then ran for his apartment.

Kevin smelled the smoke long before he rounded the corner and saw the fire engines clustered in the street, ladders and hoses deployed. His entire building was engulfed in flames. People were clustered on the sidewalk, some just rubbernecking, some covered in soot and wrapped in municipal blankets.

Just over his shoulder, he heard someone laugh, and he whirled around. No one behind him was laughing; they were just staring at him with frightened eyes and sidling away. Kevin shoved his hand into his pocket and felt the now-familiar faceted square.

This time, he made his way down to the stadiums, trotting down to the street where he'd lifted the pendant in the first place. He jogged the full length of the street without recognizing the woman's house. He took a deep breath and jogged back down again, slower this time. All the houses looked the same. He knew it wasn't the one with the geraniums or the one with the green door or an end unit. But that still left over a dozen houses, and they all looked the same. Kevin started to hyperventilate and run his hands through his hair. What was he supposed to do when all the houses looked the same? If he dropped the pendant in the wrong mailbox, it would just wind up back in his pocket anyway.

Kevin tipped back his head and howled. He took off down the middle of the street screaming, "Where are you? I want to give it back! Please, let me give it back!" over and over. The lights in most of the houses came on, people peering around their curtains, but no one came out. It didn't take the police long to get there, lights on but no sirens. This was a rich neighborhood, after all.

He saw the lights, and he dropped to his knees in the middle of the street panting. An officer got out of the squad car, shining his bright flashlight on Kevin. "Have you been drinking tonight, sir?"

Kevin shook his head back and forth. "I just want to give it back. I just want to give it back."

"I'm afraid you'll have to come with me, sir," the officer said.

Behind them, somewhere a car door shut, and he could hear a woman's heels click clacking on the pavement toward him.

"It's okay, Officer," said a woman's voice. "He's my cousin, and he's staying with me until we can get him into a residential treatment program. You know..."

Kevin looked up to see the woman who always worked late and on weekends. She was twirling her finger next to her temple and giving the officer a wink.

Scrambling to his feet, he exclaimed, "It's you!"

"Of course it's me, Randy," she said in a deliberately slow voice, taking both of his hands in hers. "I'm going to take you home now."

The officer smiled and tipped his hat to the woman. "Try to keep him under control, ma'am. Good luck." And he walked back to his cruiser where his partner radioed back to base about the non-disturbance disturbance.

The woman put her arms around Kevin's shoulders and started to lead him back to her house, looking over her shoulder at the cops pulling away.

"I just want to give it back," Kevin whispered in her ear.

The woman waited until the cops had turned the corner, then stopped and held out her hand. "Give it to me," she said.

Kevin scrabbled in his pocket and dumped the canary diamond pendant into her outstretched hand. He wiped his hands on the back of his pants.

The woman held the pendant up and let it dangle in the sticky night air. "You've been very bad, Uncle Louie. It's not nice to play with other people like that." She shook the gem a little.

Kevin stood staring at her with his mouth hanging open.

The woman tilted her head to the side and smiled. "When my Uncle Louie died, my Aunt Hazel had his ashes squeezed into a diamond, this one." She jiggled the canary diamond pendant at Kevin. He took a step back.

"Apparently," the woman said. "Part of his soul got trapped in the gem, and he's been haunting us every since. He's a real practical joker, as I'm sure you've noticed." All the metal trashcan lids up and down the block rattled on the top of their cans.

He took another step back and started shaking his head.

"It was kind of nice to have a few days off from him," the woman said. "So, if you ever want to babysit my Uncle Louie again, c'mon by."

Kevin turned and bolted with the woman's laughter following him into the night.

# The Talent of Water

"I wonder what would be worse: getting evicted or risk living with one of these pieces of work." Cassie muttered over her legal pad of notes. She leaned back and ran her hands through her dreads.

There was the Macho Man, who wanted to bring his pet boa constrictor, with no tank, and who was already planning on rearranging the living room to make room for his weight machine. There was the Twig, a skinny girl desperately in need of a sandwich, who wanted Cassie to float the first month's rent to her on the promise that she would pay double the next. And the sweet Space Cadet, who seemed like she couldn't keep her brain on planet Earth for more than ten minutes at a time but who might just be the best bet for a non-creepy roommate to pay rent reliably. Cassie had to get someone into the second bedroom soon. Baltimore landlords, especially her's, were rarely forgiving, and her thin savings account was just about to give out. There had been just barely enough to cover the two months since her last roommate moved out without warning.

She was holding her head in her hands and contemplating the benefits of homelessness when there was a knock at the door. Hauling herself to her feet, she said under her breath, "Oh joy, who can it be? An axe murderer maybe? Just to round things out, you know."

Cassie peered through the peephole and saw a blurry, waif-thin figure, most likely female and not too threatening. She took a deep breath, plastered a fake smile on her face, and opened the door. The woman's blonde hair hung around her face in strings, like she had just stepped out of a pool. Her eyes, set in a delicate and pretty face, were deeply shadowed, as if from grief or lack of sleep. She was short, barely making Cassie's shoulder, and she looked dazed and hopeless. There was a large, old-fashioned sea bag slumped at her feet.

"Cassiopeia Woodward?" the young woman's voice was low and musical. Without knowing why, Cassie's fake smile melted into a real one as she nodded.

"My name is Kendra Visola. I've come about the room for rent?" Even though her voice quivered, it was still beautiful, and Cassie found herself stepping aside and welcoming her guest, dismissing the potential danger of a stranger. They left the sea bag by the door, and both women settled at the kitchen table.

"Would you like some tea?" offered Cassie.

Kendra shook her head. "The room is $800 a month?" She paused. "I can pay in cash, right now." She dug into the satchel-like purse slung over her shoulder and produced a wad of damp hundred dollar bills.

"Don't you want to see the room first at least?" Cassie straightened out the crumpled money. Kendra's shoulders rounded in, and she seemed to disappear into herself.

"It doesn't matter." Her voice was solemn and soft. Cassie immediately felt the need to protect the slender woman, although she could not explain why.

"Well, okay, roomie," she chirped, trying to be cheerful. "I can show you your new digs. We'll have to share a bathroom; I hope you don't mind. Usually I do more checks, like credit and criminal background, but I've got a good vibe about you." Cassie reached forward and impulsively grabbed Kendra's hand. It was frigid and damp. She tried not to let the shock show on her face when she pulled away, and she grabbed the sea bag and started dragging it back to the second bedroom.

Kendra followed behind her, looking lost.

"My last roommate left behind her bed and her dresser... well, all of her furniture really. If you don't want it, you can just get rid of it." Cassie couldn't figure out why she was chattering away. It was not her usual nature to babble.

"That's fine," said Kendra. "I don't have any furniture anyway. I'll just use it." The beauty of Kendra's voice washed away any nervousness Cassie felt and replaced it with little waves of joy.

Later that evening, Cassie sat on the edge her bed and wondered just what she had done. Kendra had disappeared into her room and hadn't spoken all evening. She refused to let Cassie help her unpack. The longer Cassie went without hearing Kendra's voice, the less sure she was that she'd made the right decision in her choice of roommate. But at least the rent was paid, in cash, and Cassie wasn't afraid that her roommate would assault her in the middle of the night.

The next morning, Cassie scrambled eggs and fried bacon, hoping to lure her roommate out. Sure enough, Kendra emerged wearing the same rumpled t-shirt and jeans she'd been wearing the day before. She sniffed the air.

"What is that?"

"Breakfast," Cassie said cheerfully. "Do you like coffee or tea?"

"I don't know."

"Okay, well, I'll make tea since that's what I usually have." Her brow furrowed in confusion. "Just relax. Everything will be ready in a few minutes. I've got to warn you, though... I don't do this every morning. Sometimes you'll have to make your own breakfast."

Kendra nodded as she slid into a chair at the kitchen table and folded her hands into her lap.

When Cassie put the plates on the table, Kendra just stared her food. Cassie had already shoveled down several bites before she noticed.

"What's wrong?" she mumbled around a mouthful of egg and toast.

"What is it?" Kendra whispered.

"Are you serious?" Cassie wiped her mouth with a napkin. "It's breakfast, just like I said. Haven't you ever had eggs and bacon?"

Kendra shook her head. "My mother didn't cook much. We mostly ate fish and kelp."

"Oh God, are you on some kind of special diet? Did I just give you something that grosses you out? I'm so sorry." A bright red flush showed under the mahogany tone of her skin.

"Oh no, you are very kind. Mother just never fixed anything like this. What is this again?" Kendra pointed to the bacon.

"That's bacon," said Cassie. "And the fluffy yellow stuff is scrambled eggs, and the crunchy triangles are toast. Most people put butter and jelly on their toast, but I like mine dry."

"Then I will try it dry, too." Kendra began to eat, small bites at first, but then with great relish. She seemed to particularly like the bacon.

While Cassie was showing Kendra how to wash the breakfast dishes, the phone rang.

"Mmmhmm," she said after a moment of silence. "I think we might be able to squeeze her in this Tuesday afternoon, and then once Mrs. Arnold delivers, we can put her in that Wednesday morning slot." She listened again.

"Sure, we can do the water birth. I've got all the equipment." She paused again.

"Okay, Susan, I'll see you Monday. Thanks for holding down the fort." She cradled the receiver and turned to Kendra, who was up to her elbows in suds.

"You know," Cassie said. "I usually ask this before I rent to anyone, but where are you working? I mean, I just need to know you've got some steady income for rent."

Kendra flushed and stared down at the half-scrubbed skillet in her hands. "I don't have a job yet. But you needn't worry about the money," she said, then looked at Cassie. "Mother gave me some, enough for a while, before I left. I will find a job before it runs out."

"Okay," Cassie nodded. "What kind of work are you looking for? Maybe I can help you find a job."

"I don't know," Kendra mumbled as she returned to scrubbing. "I don't have any talents."

"Oh, I'm sure you have some kind of talent. Everybody has at least one thing they do well."

"I have no talents." Her voice was bitter as she placed the clean skillet into the drainer. "Mother told me so."

"Oh, well." Cassie shoved her hands in her pockets, embarrassed that she seemed to have uncovered some long standing wound. "I'm sure there's something you can do."

Kendra shrugged and turned her attention to the plates.

"Hey." Cassie's eyes brightened. "Our office assistant at the birthing center where I'm a midwife just quit. It's a lot of mindless stuff, like filing, answering phones, running errands, that sort of thing, but it's work."

Kendra gave a short nod. "I'm sure it will be fine. Thank you for your kindness."

The silence was only broken by fitful splashing as Kendra continued to work on the dishes, and Cassie groped for something to break the thick tension in the room. "You have such a pretty name. Where does it come from?"

"It means 'magical water baby,' but I've never quite lived up to it," Kendra said without turning to face Cassie, furiously scrubbing at the plates. Cassie wandered away, wondering if her new roommate had been raised in some weird vegan cult and if she had better lock her bedroom door at night or put the local psych ward on speed dial.

Polly Brennan arrived 25 minutes early for her appointment with a thick folder containing all her medical records, right back to her birth in an army hospital in Germany.

"I'm sorry." She laughed. "I know I'm over prepared. I guess it comes from being an army brat, then an army wife. You have to carry your life with you."

"This is good." Cassie flipped through the voluminous record. "This way, we know we don't miss a thing. The more information, the better. So, I hear from Susan that you'd like to try a water birth."

"Mmmhmm. I think it would be better for the baby, you know? To go from one water environment to another." Polly patted her round, six-month belly.

"That is the theory. We can talk a little more about the pros and cons later, just to make sure you're making an informed decision for you and your baby. Right now, I'd like to take a quick ultrasound so we can get a look at the little one."

"No problem." Polly as she settled back on the exam table and pulled up her shirt to reveal her stomach. "I also have all the ultrasounds from the birthing center in California so you can see the development, if you like."

"That would be nice." Cassie said as she pulled on a set of latex gloves and squeezed a generous dollop of warmed jelly onto Polly's belly. "So how come you didn't stay out in California to have the baby?"

"Chad and I already had everything in motion for the move before I found out I was pregnant. And with him shipping out to Iraq and me being dependent on base housing, there just wasn't any way we could stop the process. All of my family is in Nebraska anyway, so with Chad in Iraq, I'd be going it alone whether I was here or in California."

"Oh no... Please don't tell me you're doing this all by yourself."

"I'm not totally alone." Polly laughed. "I have you, don't I? Seriously, the base wives are awesome; they've all been checking in on me.

And my mom is going to fly in after the baby is born to help me for the first few weeks. It's just that she doesn't get a lot of vacation time, and we both figured that was the best way for her to use it."

There was a timid knock at the door. Cassie raised her eyebrow at Polly, who said, "It's fine. It's not like anything is showing."

"C'mon in," Cassie called.

Kendra poked her head in the door. "Susan asked me to give you a message."

"Okay," Cassie waved her into the room. "Come on in and tell me then."

Kendra stepped into the room, her hands clasped tight in front of her. "Mrs. Zalinski would like to come in today. She tripped and hurt her ankle, and she wants to know if you could check the baby." Kendra's eyes fastened onto the grainy ultrasound screen and grew wide.

"Tell Susan that I can slip Mrs. Zalinski in around 3:00. I want to check her blood pressure and put the baby on a monitor," said Cassie.

Kendra didn't nod but stepped closer to the screen, her jaw slack. "What is it?"

"It's a baby." Polly laughed with good-humored warmth. "Haven't you ever seen one before?"

"No... Not a human one at least."

"Kendra is new to the center," Cassie explained, fumbling with the ultrasound wand and trying to cover up her astonishment over Kendra's comment. "Today is her first day."

"Today is my first day, too, Kendra, so we have something in common." Polly smiled. "Would you like to feel my stomach? The baby is really active right now, and you might get to feel him kick."

Kendra's eyes widened even more, and she sidled up to the exam table like a skittish horse. Cassie bit her lip and held her tongue; there was no reason to scare Polly over the sudden unease in her throat. Kendra reached out a tentative hand and touched Polly's sticky belly. On the screen, the women watched as the baby immediately turned and reached out a tiny hand for the exact part of Polly's belly that Kendra was touching. The little hand touched the uterine wall deliberately, slowly, and with great care. Polly could feel the baby press up against Kendra's palm.

"Well," she said. "I guess he likes you."

"He likes you, too," Kendra said as she raised her eyes to meet Polly's. "But he wishes you wouldn't eat so much spicy food. It makes him itchy, and that's why he wiggles all over when you do."

Cassie and Polly regarded Kendra in shocked silence. Kendra looked from woman to woman and finally drew her hand back. Silence hung heavy in the air.

"Maybe you should go tell Susan that Mrs. Zalinski can come in," Cassie said, her voice tight.

Kendra nodded, and she scuttled from the room. Cassie and Polly looked at each other and shared a moment of uncomfortable laughter and continued on with the appointment. Neither of them was sure what else to do.

The office was in a festive mood. One of their pro-bono cases, a 16-year-old runaway living in a church-run shelter for unwed mothers, had given birth to a healthy eight-pound nine-ounce baby girl with a thick shock of blonde hair. The birth had been relatively easy, and the girl had made it from beginning to end completely naturally, just as she had wanted. Almost every woman who worked in the birthing center had taken a turn holding her hand and coaching her breathing since the poor thing had no family and the father was long gone. Once the parish priest had settled the young mother and her new bundle into his car, the office decided it was time to kick up their heels a bit with a nice dinner and some drinks.

The sky over the harbor was gray and dark, but that did not dampen the enthusiasm of the laughing women. Even Kendra smiled and joined in the joking. The others took it as a welcome change over her usual shy and skittish demeanor. Cassie watched her from the other side of the group as she sipped her chardonnay and tried to decide if the incident with Polly and Kendra three months ago still bothered her. There had been no further incidents with Kendra touching mothers and telling them what their babies said. Kendra watched the mothers with interest, and when she thought no one was looking, she examined ultrasound pictures with great care, but she never touched anyone. She even politely demurred when invited. Cassie shrugged off her thoughts and forced herself to join in the merriment.

After dinner, one of the young apprentice midwives suggested that they go to a high-end bar at the other end of the Inner Harbor, since there was a better chance of finding good-looking, drink-buying men there. Outside, the gray sky was beginning to fulfill its promise, and the first fat drops of a mammoth rainstorm fell. The women huddled in the restaurant doorway and debated whether the bar was a good idea anymore.

"Oh, c'mon," Cassie called as she dashed into the beginnings of the rain, made brave by the extra glass of wine. "We're not made of sugar; we won't melt!"

The other women looked at each other and laughed, then followed Cassie out into the rain. They danced and skipped their way over the brickwork of the Inner Harbor promenade, playing silly games as they went. By the time they were even with the tall ship anchored in the harbor, the rain was coming down hard, and all six women were soaked to the skin. But they were still laughing, and they promised each other hot Irish Coffees to warm up. Susan was the first to spot the homeless man weaving his way to end of the ship's dock.

"Do you think we should do something about him?" She tugged Cassie's sleeve and pointed the man out.

"What? You mean like call the cops?" Cassie bit her lip as the man wobbled dangerously close to the edge of the dock.

"Something, anything," said Susan. "I don't think he's safe."

The other women gathered around Cassie and Susan, and they hugged their arms to themselves in the rain as they watched the man get closer and closer to the edge.

"Who's got a cell handy?"

The young apprentice nodded and started to dig her purse when Susan let out a little scream. The man pitched off the dock into the greasy harbor water. All timidness forgotten, the women raced to where the man fell in. The water was black and gray, tossed around in a froth from the rising storm. Dead fish and man-made debris slapped against the dock, but there was no sign of the man.

"Oh god," said Susan. "What do we do? I can't even see him."

"We call the police, just like we were about to. They'll be able to do something." Cassie nodded to the apprentice who put her cell to her ear.

"They can't get here in time! He'll drown by then, Cassie!"

"What are we supposed to do, Susan? Are you strong enough to swim against that?" Cassie gestured to the churning water. "And drag up twice your weight in passed out drunk?"

Susan looked at Cassie with her arms held out and eyes full of tears, mouth working on words that wouldn't come out. Kendra slid past the two women and up to the edge of the dock. She drew a deep breath and squared her shoulders, rolling her head from side to side to loosen her neck.

"Kendra!" cried Cassie, reaching out her arm. "No! Don't go in the water!"

But Kendra did not dive into the water. Instead, she pushed her palms out in front of her and murmured under her breath in a musical language no one could understand. The harbor water shifted down and out, creating a waterless void under Kendra's feet. It was impossible to tell if the wetness on Kendra's face was rain or sweat, but her jaw was clenched, and the cords stood out on her neck in obvious strain. As more water flowed away from the void, Cassie, Susan, and the other women could see all the detritus that gathered on the bottom of the Baltimore City harbor - lumpy tires, rusted oil drums, jagged spikes of wood that might once have been a hull - all covered in algae and mud. Draped over this mass of rotting junk was the drunken homeless man, choking on lungs full of water but still alive. The cell phone slid out of the young apprentice's hand and clattered onto the dock.

"Please," Kendra gasped through gritted teeth. "Someone go get him. I can't hold it forever."

The women worked together and climbed down the access ladder nailed to a piling, then slogged through the muck to the man. It took three of them to pick him up, but they made it to the ladder and heaved in concert until they had him flopped belly down onto the dock. The birthing center women hauled themselves up and sprawled all over the planking, gasping for air and covered with mud and muck. When the last of them was finally panting on the dock, Kendra let out her breath and fell to her knees. The water rushed back into the void with a crash and shook the dock. In the distance, they could hear sirens. Susan's training as a registered nurse kicked in, and she checked the man for signs of life. He was breathing in ragged, wet gasps, and his pulse was thin and thready, but he was alive.

Cassie rolled over onto her elbow and said, "Kendra, what the hell was that?" But Kendra was already gone. Everyone else had been so absorbed in catching her breath that no one had seen her go.

It took Cassie over an hour to get back to the row house apartment, even though the trip should have only taken 15 minutes at most. The police wanted to talk to her, and cabs were scarce in the rain, but she finally made it.

"Kendra?" she called as she tossed her keys and wet purse on the kitchen table. There was no answer.

Cassie peered into Kendra's bedroom, which was dark and empty. She saw the bathroom door was shut and knocked. "Kendra?"

She waited, but there was still no answer. Cassie strained to hear with her ear next to the door. She thought she heard a soft splash and knocked again. There was still no answer, but the door swung open easily when she gave it a little push.

Kendra's sodden clothes were strewn all over the floor. There was another splash, so Cassie looked into the giant, antique cast-iron claw foot tub that dominated their bathroom. It was full to the brim, and every so often, a little bit sloshed over the side, accounting for the occasional splash. Kendra lay on the bottom of the tub, on her back, naked, completely submerged with her eyes shut and arms crossed over her chest.

Cassie shrieked, and Kendra's eyes flew open. Cassie fell back on her bottom and began to crab walk backwards.

Kendra shot up out of the water and leaned over the side of the tub reaching for her roommate. "Wait, wait. Please don't go."

"What the hell? Are you trying to kill yourself or something?"

"No." Kendra sank down into the tub and rested her arms on the edge. "Water just comforts me when I get stressed."

"Trying to drown yourself comforts you? That's sick. You need help."

"I can't drown, Cassie. Mermaids, even just part mermaids, can't drown."

"If this is a joke, it's not funny... especially not after tonight."

Kendra extended a dripping hand. "Let me show you something."

After a long moment, Cassie crawled forward and took Kendra's ice cold hand. Kendra placed it on the side of her smooth, slender neck. Cassie's dark fingers stood out in sharp contrast to Kendra's milk-white skin.

"Feels normal, right?" Kendra looked to Cassie, who nodded.

"Stay with me," Kendra said. She held Cassie's hand to her neck and sank back into the tub, pulling Cassie up into a squatting position. Kendra slipped under the water and stayed there. Cassie felt something tickle her palm, but Kendra held her hand fast for a moment, then let Cassie pull her hand away from the woman's neck. She kept her fingers twined with Cassie's.

Cassie saw what had tickled her palm. Gills. Bright red gills breaking the smooth white skin of Kendra's neck, gently opening and closing. She gasped and put her fingers back to Kendra's neck, probing the fluttering gills with her fingertips. She stayed that way for several minutes, breathing in and out, feeling the gills tickle her fingertips until she fully realized that Kendra really was breathing underwater. She yelped and yanked her hand away, falling back on her bottom again.

Kendra rose out of the water, holding her shoulders. "Please don't hate me. I couldn't stand that. You're the first person who ever believed in me." Tears joined the bathwater coursing down her face.

"What? How?" Cassie stammered.

"My father was a sailor, and my mother is the Queen of the Mermaids," Kendra whispered as she shut her eyes and dropped her chin to her chest. "I was born without a tail, and normally that would mean I'd be abandoned on land by my mermaid mother, but since I had royal blood, they let me stay in the undersea kingdom. They were hoping I would overcome my disability and grow a proper tail. When that didn't happen, Mother was forced to banish me, and here I am."

Silence stretched between the two women, the only sound in the bathroom the steady drip of water from the lip of the tub. Both women startled when the phone rang. On auto-pilot, Cassie pulled herself up off the floor and answered it.

"I'll be there in twenty minutes," she said at the end of a brief conversation and cradled the receiver. She walked back into the bathroom. "Polly Brennan is in labor. I have to go."

"Please, let me go with you," Kendra said. "I promise I'll stay out of the way. I just don't want to be alone tonight."

Cassie bit her lip and thought a moment, then nodded. "Be ready to go in ten minutes. I need to get into some dry clothes."

Polly Brennan labored hard in the tub. Both her heartbeat and the baby's were all over the map. Cassie stepped away from the tub for a moment to whisper to Kendra, who hovered at the edge of the room.

"She's not doing well," she whispered, her lips close to Kendra's ear. "We may need to transport to the hospital. She's not going to like it, but if I give you the sign you go call the ambulance, no matter what she says."

Kendra nodded.

"I think we have some movement," called Susan from the tub. Polly let out a wet groan, sagging against the edge of the tub.

"You're doing great," Cassie said with false cheerfulness as she rubbed Polly's shoulders. "Why don't we try another round of pushing?"

Polly struggled upright and settled into more purposeful breathing. Susan and Cassie breathed rhythmically right along with her, chanting encouragement. Even Kendra, from her place against the wall, breathed in time with the other women. Polly strained and screamed, throwing her head back against Cassie's shoulder.

"I think he's coming! One more big push!" cried Susan.

Polly tucked her chin into her chest and bore down, cheeks puffing and eyes screwed shut. The baby finally slid into Susan's hands. She pulled him up from the water and hooked the mucus out of his mouth with her finger. But he didn't cry.

Susan looked up at Cassie with fear in her eyes, then started to work on chest compressions.

"What's wrong? Why isn't he crying?" Polly's voice screeched over the edge of hysteria.

Cassie worked to calm Polly, and Susan worked the limp body in her arms. But no matter what she did, he didn't cry or draw breath.

"Oh my god, what's wrong with my baby?" shrieked Polly.

Susan held the silent child in her arms, the words of condolence already on her lips, when Kendra slid into the tub next to her and held out her arms.

"Here," she said. "Let me try."

Susan handed her the child in numb silence, while Cassie clutched a sobbing Polly in her arms. Polly was trying to struggle to see her baby, but Cassie held her tight.

"What are you doing?" she hissed, but Kendra disappeared beneath the water with the boy without sparing her so much as a glance.

Kendra lay on her side on the bottom of the pool, curling into a fetal ball as she drew the child close to her. Cassie and Susan could see her put her head close to the boy's head, and her lips were moving. Little bubbles broke the surface of the water. The only sounds to be heard were Polly's sobs. Long minutes passed, and Polly's crying slowed.

"Where's my baby?" Her voice was resigned. "I want to hold him at least." Her voice was muffled by Cassie's shoulder, who held her there.

Susan and Cassie looked at each other, then down at the bottom of the pool where Kendra still lay, whispering into the boy's ear.

"Should we?" Susan started to speak, but she stopped when she felt the water move hard against her legs.

Kendra broke the surface with the child on her shoulder. His first breath rasped against the silence, and he let out a huge, hiccupping cry. Polly pulled away from Cassie and immediately reached out her arms for her son.

"It's a miracle," she whispered as she drew her crying son to her chest. She looked up at Cassie and Susan, laughing. "I thought he wasn't breathing there for a minute."

Cassie patted Polly's shoulder. "Sometimes it just takes them a minute to get started... the shock of birth and all that, you know."

"Uh-huh." Polly only paid half attention to Cassie's words, immersed in the wonder of the child in her arms. She counted fingers and toes and eyes and lips. Her fingertips drifted softly over his face. "Well, would you look at that, a birthmark."

Polly's fingers traced the spiral pattern of nautilus shell by her son's ear where Kendra's lips had touched him.

Cassie helped Kendra out of the birthing tub, while Susan tended to the new mother and child, cleaning and comforting them both.

"Your mother was wrong, you know," she said as she wrapped her friend in a towel. "You do have talent... the talent of water."

Kendra looked up at Cassie with tears in her eyes. "You think that could be useful?"

"I think it could be very useful. In fact, you might want to consider becoming a midwife specializing in water birth. You could be my apprentice." Cassie squeezed Kendra's shoulder.

"I'd like that."

"But you might want to hide those gills before they see." Cassie cast a pointed glance over to Polly and Susan.

Kendra slung the towel around her neck, and they both turned to cleaning up.

# Bad for Business

Roberto Perez pawed through his great-grandfather's boxes of personal effects without much interest. The attic was stuffy and dusty, and he'd rather be on the golf course or taking a nap.

"Tell me why I'm doing this again?" he complained to his wife, who was also going through boxes. Roberto stifled a yawn.

"We are doing this," Angela said, making sure he heard that she was part of the venture. "Because donating some things to the dental museum will look good for us, and they're bound to mention you as the donor in the exhibit. Good advertising."

"It's only the Baltimore one, for cripes sake," he muttered and shoved one box to the side in favor of another.

"You work in Baltimore, Bert. Giving something to the museum in New York or L.A. wouldn't do you much good. Your customers are here." Angela glanced over at her husband.

"Stop pouting," she said. "It's good for business to look like the generous benefactor. And besides, it'll clear a lot of this old junk out of the attic. I don't know about you, but I'd love to have some more storage space."

Roberto merely grunted.

"Fine. If you're going to be such a whiner, do it yourself. I have better things to do," Angela said as she dusted off her pants and headed for the pull down stairs.

"But Angie, sweetheart!" Roberto protested.

"Don't sweetheart me," she groused as she headed down the stairs. "And make sure you get rid of any old tools of his, too; they're just creepy."

Roberto sulked for a few minutes, waiting for Angela to relent and come back up the stairs, but five minutes passed, and she didn't come back. About ten minutes after she left the attic, Roberto heard her car start and back out of the driveway. Roberto cursed to himself.

"Probably going shopping," he muttered, leaning his forehead against the wall. His eyelids began to flutter shut, and he yawned again. "I'm going to need more patients to cover this bill."

He pushed himself away from the wall with a grunt and surveyed the attic. It was full of the detritus of four generations of dental practice, of which his great-grandfather had been the first. Perez Dentistry had built itself up from a little hovel in the Spanish ghetto, eventually moving to the gleaming offices he now had out on Rolling Road, with the finest equipment he could afford and a full patient roster every week. Roberto was sure his great-grandfather would have been pleased that so many of his patients were rich and white. He still did some pro bono work for ghetto kids, but he kept it to a minimum; just enough to make him look good, not enough to hit the balance sheet too hard.

"Let's get this over with," he said to himself, then sighed.

One of the first things to go should be his great-grandfather's first dentist's chair. Roberto yanked the sheet off of it and promptly had a sneezing fit from the flying dust. It was plain black leather, cracking, almost medieval looking compared to the sleek blue and chrome models he'd just had installed in his office. This was the first real chair his great-grandfather had been able to afford. The first Dr. Perez had practiced for years using plain kitchen chairs before he could buy this one, used, from a white dentist who was getting an upgrade. It was the only chair any of the Perez dentists had bothered to keep when it stopped being useful. All the others had been sold or given away. It was also huge. Getting rid of it would clear out plenty of the space Angela said she wanted.

Roberto grabbed it by its footrest and started to pull it toward the stairs. It came slowly, scraping against the wood floor and leaving a bright trail through the thick dust. He changed his grip and pulled harder, inching it along just a bit more. Wiping the sweat that popped out on his brow, he stood to examine the situation and see if there was a better way to move it. Grabbing it by the main seat rather than the footrest might give him a bit more leverage. He wrapped his hands around the chair's seat and pulled but yanked his hand back as something hard bit into the soft center of his palm.

Looking more closely, he could see the corner of something poking out from the leather and horsehair stuffing. It was hard to get a grip on the tiny corner, but he kept working it, bit by bit, and see-sawed it out enough to get a good grip. By now, he could see it was some sort of book, a very old book, that someone had hidden in the chair a long time ago. He could also see that he was going to have to cut the leather to get the book the rest of the way out.

After running down to the kitchen for a knife, Roberto hoped he could get it back in the block before Angela realized he'd used her precious high-end blade for something so rough. Carefully, he sliced where the leather met wood at the edge of the chair. He didn't want to do the kind of damage that would make the museum turn down his donation. He slid the book from its hiding place and brushed away stray horsehairs. There was nothing stamped on its red leather cover, nothing to hint at its contents. The leather creaked as he flipped it open.

It was his grandfather's spidery script that covered each page in cramped rows. As he began to read, he saw that it was a diary from when his great-grandfather and grandfather first moved their father-son dental practice to real offices on the nice side of town. There was a lot of detail about what they'd bought to furnish the place, how they convinced new patients to try the Latino dentist, and how happy they both had been. Roberto flipped through the pages faster, disappointed that it wasn't anything more interesting, when a drawing in the middle of all the cramped writing caught his eye.

It was a small, slender figure with wings and a small sack in her hands. Roberto shook his head in wonder; such a fanciful thing was far out of character for his straitlaced grandfather. All around the drawing, following the edges of it like a river to a bank, was more of his grandfather's cramped writing. It explained that the tooth fairy was real, and that in fact, her relationship with humans was a symbiotic one. She took the teeth and left money for the children, but she lived on the magic stored in the teeth she took. Her preference was children's teeth because the magic was stronger in the innocents, but adult teeth would do in a pinch if she was really hungry. Without any teeth to feed on, the tooth fairy would eventually wither away and die.

"This is nuts." Roberto snapped the book shut. "Grandpa was a loon." He laughed as he levered himself up off the floor. Sliding the slender volume in his back pocket, he went back to the task of moving the chair. By the time Angela returned, laden down with shopping bags from the mall, Roberto had a pile ready to donate to the museum, including the old chair, some of the vicious looking tools his great-grandfather had used, and papers and log books about patients and the daily minutia of dental practice.

Later that evening, when Angela was already in bed, and Roberto was getting undressed, the book fell out of his back pocket onto the bathroom floor. He picked it up and turned it around in his hands, wondering if he should have chucked it in the box of things for the museum, but then he thought the better of it. It wouldn't do for any of the members of Perez Family Dentistry to be seen as crazy. That would be bad for business.

He flipped the book open back to the drawing again, wondering just how crazy his grandfather had been. Further on in the book, nestled between an account of a wisdom tooth extraction and a really bad abscess, Roberto found another mention of the tooth fairy. Here, his grandfather wrote about finding a way to extract the magic, just like the tooth fairy did, and use it for himself. It involved grinding the tooth to a fine powder while saying certain incantations, then ingesting the tooth. He made a face at the thought of eating someone else's tooth. But the entry went on to talk about how well it worked, how he felt like he had boundless energy after the spell was done, and that was just with a teenager's wisdom tooth. How much more could be gained by a small child's tooth, especially the first one?

Roberto kept flipping through the book to see if his grandfather had ever continued the experiment with children's teeth. Indeed, in an entry about a week and a half later, Roberto found it. A young boy had come in with a sports injury, fast ball to the face, and Dr. Perez had to pull six teeth, some broken, some merely cracked. It was easy to pocket the most pristine one and give the boy the other damaged ones to put under his pillow for the tooth fairy. After Roberto's grandfather worked the spell for the boy's tooth, he didn't need to sleep for a week, and he still felt full of energy and vigor, and there was no crash at the end. He just went back to his normal sleeping schedule. Unfortunately, there seemed to be an addictive component to it.

The journal went on to detail Roberto's grandfather's increasingly desperate ploys to get teeth from his patients. Sometimes, he just palmed them, and if the patient noticed, he would lie and say it must have fallen off the tray. For a while, he told his child patients that teeth pulled in the dentist's office didn't count, that the tooth fairy didn't want them. Then he got bold, and he told the children he was an agent of the tooth fairy. He would give them each a shiny silver dollar, four times than what most parents were giving as tooth fairy payments in those days, and pocket the tooth. Everyone was happy; no one was the wiser.

Until Roberto came on one short entry, in a hurried scrawl by itself in the middle of the page. The letters were large and jagged, very much unlike his grandfather's usual tight, neat script.

Don't do it. Don't do what I have done. THEY will get you - no matter where you hide.

After that, there was no more mention of keeping teeth or the rituals that accompanied them. Roberto tried to parse out the sentences for any tiny, hidden clue, but it just wasn't there. The journal finished with the same boring minutia it started with.

The museum sent Roberto a letter of profuse thanks for his generous donation, along with two year-long passes for him and his wife. They planned to build a whole new exhibit around what Roberto had given them, all about the infancy of dental care in Baltimore, with a focus on the poorer end of town. There was going to be a grand gala opening in two months time, and they hoped the couple would join them as guests of honor. Roberto gave the letter to Angela, since she took care of all of the social engagements, and went off to the office for another boring day of mucking around in other people's mouths.

The schedule for the day was the usual mix: cleanings for adults, tightening up some teens' braces, and few check-ups for children. Everything went as usual until the last appointment of the day, a back-to-school check-up. Little Sally Swanson was a squirmer and a screamer, and she hated dentists. Roberto hated dealing with patients like this, but he had bills to pay, especially since Angela had just decided she wanted a new car, so he gritted his teeth and got on with it. Sally had one tooth that was hanging on by a thread.

"Sally," said Roberto. "You have one tooth that looks like it's about to come out on its own. Would you like me to help it along?"

"No!" shouted Sally.

"You could put it under your pillow for the tooth fairy tonight. Wouldn't that be nice?"

"No!" shouted Sally.

"Let the nice doctor do what he needs to do," said her mother.

"No!" shouted Sally.

"It's okay, Mrs. Swanson." He sighed and rubbed the bridge of his nose. "I'll just examine the rest of her teeth, and I'm sure that tooth will fall out soon on its own. I'd just keep an eye on it."

Sally squirmed as he examined the rest of her teeth and pushed Roberto's thumb into the one that had been hanging on for dear life. She screeched and bit his thumb. Roberto yelped and pulled his hand away.

Sally began to wail. "You did it on purpose!"

"No, I didn't," said Roberto as he dropped her tooth on the exam tray and inspected his glove for any holes.

"I'm so sorry, Dr. Perez. I don't know what's gotten into her." Mrs. Swanson gathered her little girl up into her arms.

"It's fine, Mrs. Swanson. She didn't even break the glove, see?" He held up his hand to prove it to her. "But I think we're done here. All the rest of her teeth look fine. You can see the receptionist on the way out for the bill and to make your next appointment. See you in six months." Roberto smiled, but Sally wailed louder.

In the silence of the office after the Swanson's left, Roberto let his shoulders slump forward and wondered, yet again, what he was doing in dentistry. It certainly wasn't something he loved. But the money was good, that was for sure; if only it didn't leave him so damn tired all the time. His eyes fell on Sally Swanson's baby tooth, sparkling against the blue paper liner of the exam tray. He told himself that he was just going to hold it for her until she came for her next appointment. Surely, she would want to put it under her pillow. At least, that's what he told himself as he slipped it into his pocket.

It took Roberto a little over a week to drum up the courage to try his grandfather's energy cure. The thought of swallowing little Sally Swanson's tooth still made his stomach churn, but he was just so damn tired. Twice that week, he'd fallen asleep in his car in the parking lot after leaving his office, hand on the ignition. He didn't wake up until Angela called his cell, worried out of her mind that he'd been in an accident or was cheating on her. He needed to do something, and coffee and energy drinks just weren't cutting it anymore.

He waited until Angela scheduled a night out with her girlfriends and saw her off at the door with more than his usual cheer. There would be more than just pizza and beer tonight. Tonight was about more than just watching a game uninterrupted. After he was sure Angela was down the street and she wasn't coming back for something she forgot, Roberto raced up the stairs to the bathroom two at a time. He took the journal and Sally Swanson's tooth, wrapped in a plastic sandwich baggie, from their hiding place in the back of the one drawer he was allowed to have in the bathroom. He shivered a little bit, but he was determined.

Roberto followed his grandfather's directions to a tee - the grinding, the incantations, suspending the ground up tooth in a glass of milk and drinking down without taking a breath. He waited a second, glass in hand in the middle of the kitchen, waiting to see if he felt any different. At first he didn't, but then the warmth began to blossom in his stomach and spread out from there. He felt awake, energetic, ready to conquer the world.

The dentist didn't sleep for a week and a half. He worked not only all his regular appointments but extra last minute call-ins as well. The office staff didn't like having to stay late, but Roberto didn't mind since he felt so chipper and perky. At home, he made love to his wife three times that week, instead of his usual one, and he finished all the little honey-do tasks around the house she'd been nagging him about for months. And while she slept, he crept down to the basement and worked on his model airplanes. He loved those models but rarely had any time to touch them since he was so tired all the time.

Just like his grandfather had written, there was no crash. Roberto just went back to his regular nightly sleep cycle. But there was a hunger, a hunger for the boundless energy, a hunger to get everything finished and not leave the list half done. He tried to think of ways to get teeth without arousing suspicion that he was some kind of freak. That would be bad for business.

It wasn't hard to get adult teeth. When he pulled those, most of the time the adults didn't want them anyway. It was easy to pocket them and take them home and perform the ritual. But the adult teeth were only good for a 24 to 48 hour blast of energy at best. Sometimes, he could sneak wisdom teeth from extractions, which mostly came from older teenagers and young twenty-somethings. When the patient asked for the teeth as a souvenir, Roberto would give them two or three, but hold back one or two and tell the patient that he'd had to crush the tooth to get it out. Since the patients were inevitably loopy from anesthesia, he got away with it every time. But even those teeth did not pack the punch of a young child's baby tooth. The wisdom teeth gave him three or four days of blessed productivity, not the week or week and a half he hungered for. The children's teeth were hard to come by, and every single brat wanted to take it home to give to the tooth fairy.

In the end, Roberto resorted to the ploy his grandfather used to such great advantage: he pretended to be an agent for the tooth fairy. He kept a stack of crisp five dollar bills in the pocket of his lab coat, and he presented one for every baby tooth he could wheedle out of his patients. The parents were pleased to not have to go through a sleepy midnight ritual, and the children seemed especially pleased over the higher payout. Roberto had collected quite a little cache of teeth, more than enough to keep him going for months before anything went wrong.

He was in the basement on a Wednesday night, working on a new model, when he heard tip-tapping on the small window above his head. At first, he thought it was just the wind, but the knocking continued even when the night was still. Roberto stood on his tip toes, with his fingertips on the high windowsill, to see out the glass. There was a tiny, pinched face pressed up against the glass and teeny little balled fists beating on the window. It looked exactly like the drawing in his grandfather's journal.

As if in a dream, he undid the latch and tilted the window up. The little woman tumbled in and fell on his workbench, nearly breaking her wings off in the process. She laid there on the workbench of a moment, looking dazed and confused, then pushed herself up on her hands and knees. She shook her head and looked up at Roberto, her mouth working like a fish out of water.

"Please, whatever it is you are doing, please stop," she begged. "I'm starving. Please, I'm starving."

The little woman did indeed look painfully thin. Her collarbone jutted out, and her fingers looked more like bony claws.

"Are you?" Roberto swallowed. "Are you the tooth fairy?"

"Yes," she said. "I don't know what you're doing, but I haven't gotten any teeth for weeks, and there were only a few before that. I'm starving!"

"What do you want me to do about it?"

"Let me have my harvest!" she cried and beat her diminutive fists against the workbench. "Would you starve another living creature?" Her eyes were desperate, and she was panting.

Roberto looked toward the stairs, thinking of his wife, but at this hour, she was fast asleep in their second-floor bedroom. He reached behind a box of unfinished models and pulled out a mason jar full of teeth. He took out a small incisor and rolled it across the workbench to the fairy.

She screeched and pounced on it, sucking it until it turned black. She licked her lips. "More."

Roberto rolled her a molar this time. She sucked that one down and begged for more. Roberto rolled her half a dozen teeth, and with each tooth, she grew fuller, her wings perked up, and her skin lost its sickly pallor.

"More," she begged again, holding out her wee hands.

"No," said Roberto, screwing the lid back on the jar and returning it to its hiding place. "I only gave you those because I didn't want to see you starve in front of me. Now, get out of my house and never come back." He pointed to the still open basement window.

"But, but," stammered the fairy. "You're taking my harvest. I'm going to starve."

"There are plenty of other kids in the world," said Roberto. "I'm just taking some in Baltimore; you've got the rest of the world."

"I can't go into other territories... the king would kill me," squeaked the fairy.

"Wait, there's more than one of you?"

The little fairy gasped and clapped her hands over her mouth. "I didn't say anything," she mumbled around her hands.

"Hah! So there are more than one of you!" Roberto grabbed the fairy and tossed her out the window. "Well, you can get charity from your friends, not me. Stay away from my house, or I'll rip your wings off next time."

Roberto slammed the window shut and turned the latch. Before he went back to building his model, he found another hiding place for his jar of teeth.

On Thursday night, Roberto was just unpacking a new model when he heard tip-tapping at his basement window again. He tried to ignore it, but the tip-tapper was persistent. Finally, he wrenched open the window. "I thought I told you to stay away."

But it wasn't the little woman fairy in front of him. Instead, it was a bulkier, beefier male version of fairy, mounted on the back of a white rat. Roberto couldn't decide what looked sillier to him: a tiny man with ripped delts and lats with a set of what looked like butterfly wings sprouting out of his shoulders, or the white rat, wearing a tiny bridle and saddle, waiting patiently for instructions from his rider.

"Who the hell are you?"

"I am a representative of the Tooth Fairy King, and I bring you a summons." The small man's intonation might have been sonorous and important if it hadn't been for the lack of resonance brought on by his size.

"Like I need to listen to this." Roberto drew back from the window, ready to shut it, but the fairy man urged his mount forward. Before Roberto could shut them out, both had landed on his workbench. The fairy man looked very stern. The white rat fell to cleaning his whiskers.

"You will answer the king's summons, or you will suffer the consequences," said the fairy man, and he brandished a tiny little spear.

Roberto crossed his arms and leaned back against the workbench. "What kind of consequences? I don't see that I have something to fear from someone so small." He nudged the fairy man's chest with his index fingertip, hardly putting any energy into it, but still managing to nearly knock the fairy off his rat.

The fairy man righted himself and tried to draw up some of his dignity around him. "The Tooth Fairy King has powers you can't even imagine."

Roberto made a theatrical yawn. "Whatever," he said. "I'm getting what I need, and I don't see any way you can stop me."

"You could get more," said the fairy man.

"Excuse me?"

"You could get more out of what you have," he said. "You are only taking the bare minimum of what you could have from your harvest. Not needing to rest is the very least of what you can draw."

"And the king would teach me how to get more out of the teeth?"

"If you please him." The little man leaned back in his saddle and smirked.

"Okay, fine." Roberto sighed. "I'll answer the damn summons. Where do I have to be and when?"

"Be at your museum exhibit at midnight tomorrow night. We will be there." The fairy man urged his rat forward. It scuttled across the bench and used its claws to climb up the cinderblock wall.

"Wait," said Roberto just as the fairy man and his rat were silhouetted in the open basement window. "I was just wondering... why are you riding a rat? I mean, you have wings and you can fly, right?"

"Stupid human," scoffed the fairy. "You have legs and you can walk, right? But you still ride horses." The fairy man laughed as his rat galloped away.

Roberto stood outside the museum, wondering how he was going to get inside; he was a dentist, not a cat burglar. Shifting from foot to foot, he looked at his watch again. Almost midnight. He was going to have to try something soon... What, he didn't know. But then he saw a sliver of light as a back door popped open and a little fairy woman, different from the one he'd first met, popped her head out and beckoned to him.

Without a word, he slipped through the door she offered him and followed her scampering footsteps to the exhibit made from his great-grandfather's treasures. The old dentist's chair was the centerpiece of the exhibit, lovingly restored so that the black leather fairly gleamed. In glass cases all around the edge of the room, there were the tools his great-grandfather used interspersed with examples of his journals and paperwork. Gathered on every surface were fairies, chattering among themselves.

"So, which one is the king?" Roberto looked toward his guide.

"He's not here yet, silly," she said and fluttered her way up to a case that held antique dental pliers.

Roberto was about to ask how long he had to wait when he heard tiny little trumpets sound in the corner. The king arrived in a golden, open-top carriage drawn by six pure white rats with the sleekest, shiniest fur he'd ever seen. He was surrounded by a vanguard of at least a dozen rat riders. All the fairies perched on the cases cheered and whistled, and they threw teeth. Behind the carriage, half a dozen well-muscled fairy men on foot collected up the teeth in sacks emblazoned with the royal seal. The carriage pulled up right in front of Roberto.

"Dr. Perez, I presume?" said the well-appointed little monarch.

"Yeah, that's me. So are you going to teach me your secrets, or what?"

The king frowned. "Only if you prove worthy, Dr. Perez, and haste does not speak to worthiness."

Roberto lifted his right foot just a bit and smirked. "You're small enough. I could leave your kingdom without a king if you don't teach me what I want to know."

The fairies all around him gasped and the rat riders drew up around their king, with spears pointed upward.

"I'm sorry that we weren't able to settle this like gentlefolk, Dr. Perez," the king said. "I'm afraid that you will now have to feel my wrath." He nodded to the room full of fairies and settled back in his carriage to watch.

If any one of the fairies had attacked him, Roberto would have been able to shrug it off easily, but when the whole room attacked him at once, it proved to be fairly difficult. Like a swarm of bees, they worked well together. He was sure he had done some damage based on the wee groans he could hear from the corners of the room, but the swarm still got him muscled over to the dentist's chair, where they tied him down with knots that were surprisingly secure for being tied with such small hands. Roberto began to struggle harder and scream when he heard glass break. Sure enough, the fairies hovered above him with his own great-grandfather's tools and evil grins on their faces. He clamped his mouth shut, but another half dozen fairies pulled his lips back and held them.

They started with yanking a canine. Roberto howled. He could feel the blood dribble out over his lips. Another group of fairies led forth the fairy woman he'd first met, the one he was happy to condemn to starvation. They handed her Roberto's canine, and she sucked it dry with a gleeful gleam in her eyes.

"I'm sorry, I'm sorry," he cried in the clearest mumble he could around his stretched lips. "I'll share... I promise I'll share."

But it was too late for him to share. The fairies plucked his teeth one by one and handed them all to the one who would have starved. The last thing Roberto could remember before he passed out from the pain was her little mouth laughing and her face smeared with the blood from the roots of his teeth.

The curator of the museum found him the next morning and screamed like a little girl before he called the ambulance. Roberto never would speak to anyone, not even Angela, about what happened that night. Most people assumed it was some kind of amnesia brought on by the gruesomeness of the attack. The opening of the exhibit was delayed by a week to clean up the glass and blood. When the cleaners saw all the tiny footprints in the blood, they wondered, but they kept their mouth shut. Asking strange questions would be bad for business.

# Gathering Luck

Roxie's fingertips made lazy swirls around the black box drawn on the slick paper of her calendar, and she smiled as her eyes took on a far off, dreamy look. It had been so long. Fourteen months. The last time she'd been blessed with a Friday the 13th had been that sultry day in July, and now, here it was September, with its crisp fall nights and fading Indian summer over a year later. She could finally get her life back on track. It would be a good ten years before she would have to live through another drought this long.

She was jolted out of her reverie by the tinkle of her old-fashioned bell on the front door of the shop. Heaving a sigh, she hoped it was nothing more than a couple of curious teenage girls who would browse and giggle and eventually leave with nothing more than a little incense or patchouli. Roxie tucked a curl of dishwater-blonde hair behind her ear. She could certainly use the cash from a more discerning customer. It had been very lean lately, but she didn't have the vigor necessary for such a high-energy customer right now. But the landlord wouldn't accept excuses instead of checks, so she drew herself up and plastered on a smile to go greet the customers who had wandered into her shop full of crystals, tarot cards, white sage, and all the other accoutrements considered so necessary to the New Age lifestyle.

The smile on Roxie's face became more strained when she saw who it was. Marjorie Summers, a broad-faced woman with a commanding presence, who had some sulky, but pretty, brunette in tow. Roxie's stomach churned, and she hoped that this wouldn't turn out to be the disaster she suspected it would be.

"Roxanne," burbled Marjorie. "I'm so glad you're in. I was afraid you wouldn't be and that I'd be stuck with that Caroline girl. You're so sweet to keep her on."

Roxie barely managed to keep her grimace in place as she air kissed her best customer. If it hadn't been for the gobs of money Marjorie threw around, and all the friends she'd convinced to try the shop, she would have invited her to stop coming long ago.

"You know I'm always delighted to see you, but I thought we weren't doing a reading this week. The stars are just too dark for you right now."

"Oh, I know," Marjorie's hands fluttered in the air. "But the shop is so soothing for me. So, I thought I'd just stop by and browse a little bit, and then I thought you might be able to do a reading for my friend here, Karen." She gestured to the brunette. "Maybe the stars won't be dark for her."

Roxie hoped the women didn't see her wince and wondered how she could get out of this one. Until Friday the 13th, anything she tried to "read" would be a shot in the dark. "What kind of reading were you interested in, dear?"

"I don't know. What kind do you do?" Karen yawned.

Roxie drew in her breath to answer, but Marjorie beat her to the punch. "Oh, she does just everything! Palm reading, tarot, rune stones, star charts... I don't think that there's anything Roxanne can't do." Marjorie beamed, and Karen raised an eyebrow.

"You're too kind, Marjorie." Roxie flexed her lips again.

"I don't usually go in for this kind of stuff anyway." Karen addressed Roxie. "I'm only here because Marjorie dragged me. What do you have for non-believers?"

The smile faded off of Marjorie's dark face, and she tittered uncomfortably as she cast an apologetic glance Roxie's way. But Roxie felt relieved. If Karen wasn't expecting it to be real, she could throw in enough glittering generalities to please Marjorie and send both women away satisfied.

"A three card tarot spread is the simplest, and cheapest, reading I have. And even if you don't believe what I see for you, the artwork on the cards is lovely to look at. I have a very pretty deck."

"Oh, I'm sure once you have a reading, you'll be a believer." Marjorie patted Karen's hand. "Roxanne really is wonderful."

Once Marjorie was happily browsing among the more expensive items in the store, Roxie took Karen into her curtained alcove for a reading. Karen sat back in her chair, her arms crossed over her chest, regarding her with the full weight of the hostility she'd been hiding in the shop.

"This is bullshit," she growled. "You take tons of money from my friend, and you aren't doing anything to earn it. You'd be more honest if you just begged on the streets instead of stringing along fragile people."

Roxie carefully laid her cards on the burgundy velvet cloth that covered the small table. "So why are you here if this is so awful?" Her voice was soft and devoid of emotion.

"I wanted to humor Marjorie." Her chin came up a notch.

"Then let's humor her, shall we?" Roxie said, pushing the cards toward Karen. "Shuffle these, and think about the question you want to ask."

The woman picked up the deck and shuffled the large cards with easy, economical movements. "You're not even going to try to convince me?"

Roxie sighed. "You seem pretty convinced of your righteousness, Karen. Why should I try to break my back proving things to you when the Universe will show you what you need to see when you are ready?"

"Now there's the mumbo jumbo I was looking for." She chuckled as she laid the shuffled deck onto the table.

Smiling, Roxie tilted her head to the side a little. "Now cut the deck into three piles."

"Evenly?" Karen's hand hovered above the deck.

"If that's what you want. It's important for you to cut it where it feels right to you without any direction from me."

Karen snorted and divided the deck into three haphazard, but reasonably equal, piles. Roxie's moss-green eyes twinkled with amusement as she slid smoothly into her patter.

She tapped the first stack of cards to Karen's left. "This is for the love in your life."

She tapped the cards in the center. "This is the touchstone that influences all aspects of your life."

She tapped the stack to Karen's right. "And this is your career."

Roxie returned to the first pile and neatly flipped over the top card onto the velvet, The Wheel of Fortune, reversed. She frowned. Karen saw her frown, and her arms loosened slightly as she leaned forward just a bit. Roxie flipped the next card and found The Moon. With a soft snick, the final card revealed The Chariot. Roxie had her hands flat on the table and leaned over the cards, examining them closely with her brow furrowed. Karen completely released her arms and rubbed her palms on the thighs of her jeans as she leaned in even closer.

"What is it?" Her voice was a breathless whisper.

In the back of her mind, Roxie thought, Gotcha. She looked up at Karen. "Are you a writer or some sort of performance artist?"

"No." Karen snorted and resumed her previous stance with her arms crossed even tighter.

"Hmm… well, that does make a few things clearer then." Roxie resumed her careful perusal of the cards. The other woman shifted in her chair again, and her arms loosened just ever so much.

"Well, what do they say? You know Marjorie is going to ask me." Karen rolled her eyes.

"This is the card referring to your love life," Roxie said as she tapped on The Wheel of Fortune. "Normally, this would be a very good card to get in reference to your love life, but here it's reversed so it's not so good. It warns of unexpected bad luck and a resistance to change. It's also a strong warning against gambling. Don't gamble with your heart right now, Karen, or there's bound to be bad consequences."

Karen let out a low breath and raised her right hand to her mouth as the color drained from her face. "What does the rest of it say?"

"Things are good for you in the career arena." Roxie tapped the far right card. "The Chariot shows triumph over adversity and worldly success after a period of struggle. It's a very positive and dynamic card. Just keep doing what you are doing at work, and you will be rewarded."

Karen nodded. "What else?"

"Your touchstone, the card that presides over all, is a little worrisome," Roxie started.

Karen let out a little whimper.

"The Moon is a card of illusion and changeability. In its best aspects, it represents creativity and intuition, and it's often associated with the positive aspects of the various creative endeavors. That's why I asked you if you were a writer or an artist. In its worst aspects, it can represent confusion, hiding things, and more malevolent illusions."

Karen gasped.

"But it is upright here, which means that we need to focus on the more positive aspects of the card."

"But what does it all mean?"

"Because of The Moon, you need to be careful, Karen. Things may not be what they seem, but at the same time, you need to welcome and encourage the creative aspects in your life right now. Because of the danger of the reversed Wheel of Fortune, you need to be especially careful in your love life right now. Given the positive charge of the Chariot at work, I think you should focus your energy on your career right now... rather than affairs of the heart. That's where you'll get the most positive outcome."

Karen nodded without a sound and swallowed heavily. Roxie wondered what nerve she'd managed to hit with her shot in the dark. The non-believer certainly seemed stunned, but Roxie had no idea what connections Karen was making between what she'd just said and what was going on in her real life.

"Would you like a few moments to meditate in private while I go help Marjorie?" Roxie asked her.

Karen nodded silently again, staring off into nothing.

When she finally emerged from the alcove, Roxie was ringing up Marjorie's purchases, a few books on harmless herbal remedies and some white sage smudge sticks. Karen's defenses were smoothly back in place, and she was once again the acerbic skeptic, until she looked at Roxie, who caught a glimpse of fear before Karen looked away too fast and suddenly became interested in wind chimes designed to draw fairies to a garden. Marjorie noticed nothing and left the store cheerfully chatting away with Karen in tow. Roxie rubbed the familiar edge of her counter with her thumb and wondered just what those three random cards had meant.

It was Thursday the 12th, and Roxie closed the shop early in the afternoon. She told all of her regulars it was for cleansing meditation since the stars were in the proper alignment. Most of them probably imagined her quietly breathing in and out in a lotus position with wreathes of incense all around her, but in truth, she was hot and sweaty, grunting as she hauled boxes to the roof of her building. Hard work to be sure, but she had to be ready for midnight.

Under the falling light of the setting sun, she examined the contents of the neatly laid out boxes. Lengths of pure, unused hemp rope to catch the luck of the sea and the wind, good for sea voyages and christening boats. Alligator claws, freely given, to catch money luck; these she could either keep for herself or sell in the shop for a tidy profit. A wide assortment of glass jars, vials, and test tubes with tight cork stoppers, all carefully rinsed with salt water and prayers to ensure that they were clean of all psychic vibrations and wouldn't taint the luck they caught. But the most precious of all were the witch balls. Large glass globes in a riot of colors, with a delicate web of glass strands held in their fragile walls. These were the best containers for the rarest lucks, the kind that Roxie hoarded to herself and never sold. No, what the witch balls could contain was far too precious to be traded for mere money.

After her inventory, she waited on the roof, counting the hours to midnight. Then, she would bathe in the glory that was the truth of Friday the 13th, the truth that nearly no one knew. Even though it is widely believed, it is untrue that Friday the 13th is an unlucky day. It is simply that on that day all luck becomes unmoored and flies free, and in the absence of personal luck, bad things can happen. Most of the time, the luck returns to the original owner without any problems just as the 13th shifts over to the 14th, but sometimes it attaches itself to another person, or sometimes it is captured by a determined soul. And Roxie was very determined.

She felt no guilt for the luck she captured that would never return to the original owner, since she had no luck of her own due to an unfortunate gypsy curse. Her mother had made the mistake of upsetting a traveling gypsy woman by questioning her power of second sight. So the gypsy threw a curse, but in her anger, her hand slipped, and instead of reaching the intended target, the curse settled on Roxie, still in her mother's womb. And so Roxie was born with no luck, and no way to grow any luck of her own. Fortunately for her, Madame Moraavie felt so bad over her mistake that she taught Roxie the truth of Friday the 13th and how to catch all the unmoored luck, as well as everything the gypsy knew about tarot cards, palmistry, and cold reading.

Roxie looked out over the Baltimore cityscape, jiggling from foot to foot with impatience. The bright lights of the stadiums took over the sky to the south. The Bromo Seltzer tower gave a soft purple glow to the west. As midnight drew closer, she could feel the heaviness in the air. There was a storm coming, a storm of luck. With her eyes closed, she inhaled deeply and spread her arms, swaying slightly in the cosmic wind of what was to come. There would be a heavy harvest; the luck had been leashed for too long.

At exactly one breath past midnight, the luck began to fly. Roxie whooped and began snatching containers out of the boxes. She sniffed a fresh salt breeze instead of the usual brackish harbor scents and knew there was sea luck coming first. She made coaxing sounds that sea luck would find attractive, waves and gull cries, and when it came close enough, she wrapped the hemp rope around it and tied a special knot, then another for good measure. This was strong luck, and she couldn't let it escape. The far off clinking of coins in the corner of her ear told her told her money luck was not far behind, and she dove for the box of alligator claws so she would be ready. Luck shimmered in the air on the concrete precipice of the building. She crept quietly, not wanting to scare it, then sprang forward and pinned the money luck to the concrete. She spoke the word of power, and the luck flowed into the claw and lodged there. Roxie chuckled to herself, giddy with the joy of trapping luck, when she caught the faint whiff of roses. There was love luck to be caught. A pink glass jar shaped like a heart would be perfect for this catch. Roxie called it to her with loud air kisses and breathy sighs, grinning wide as she watched the rose-scented mist slither into the bottle and fill every corner. A heavy dose of love luck indeed.

Through the night and into the pre-dawn light, she leapt and pounced her way around the roof, catching and trapping every bit of luck that wafted anywhere near her building. The boxes filled with stoppered jars and test tubes, knotted lengths of rope, and alligator claws that seemed to gleam from within. As the sun fully broke over the horizon, she stopped and stretched, looking over her boxes. She already had a decent haul, and Friday the 13th wasn't even half over. But loose luck was harder to see and smell during the daylight hours. Roxie considered things and felt it would be prudent to get some sleep during the day so she could be fresh for the easier luck hunting after sundown. She nodded to herself and took the boxes full of luck down to her apartment above the shop for safekeeping and then take a nap for herself.

The hammering on the front door of the shop jolted Roxie out of a sound sleep. She looked at the clock, 3:15 in the afternoon, and muttered darkly to herself. There were no appointments today, and she was absolutely sure that the closed sign, festooned with moons and stars, was prominent in the front window. She tossed over to her other side and pulled a pillow over her head and hoped that whoever it was would get a clue and go away. But Roxie hadn't spent any of her new caught luck yet, and the hammering continued. Finally, she threw herself out of bed, growling as she stuffed her feet into a pair of well-worn pink bunny slippers.

"I'm coming, I'm coming," she tried to shout over the banging as she shuffled into the shop, then wrenched the front door open. "What!" she shouted at the brunette skeptic, Karen.

The woman's face was wan and pale. She twisted her hands together and kept glancing up and down the street. "Can I come in? Please? I need to come in."

"I'm sorry, Karen. I'm closed today. Besides, I thought you didn't believe in all of this."

"Certain things have made me doubt my skepticism lately." Karen swallowed convulsively. "I need more information. Please, I need to come in."

"I really am closed. You can come back tomorrow." Roxie started to close the door, but some hint of movement up the street startled Karen, and she barreled past her, nearly knocking her over in the process. "What the hell!" Roxie cried.

Karen was trembling by now, and she stood in the middle of the Native American dream catcher display, hugging her arms to herself. "I need your help, Roxanne, I really do. Please, I need to have more information."

"I'm sorry, but the stars are dark today, and I couldn't possibly think of doing a reading. I'm tired, and the stars are all wrong. I wouldn't be able to see anything." Roxie glanced up the street trying to see what had spooked Karen so bad, but she saw nothing out of the ordinary.

"But you said the stars were dark when I came with Marjorie, and you saw so clearly," Karen whined.

"The stars were dark just for Marjorie that day, not for everyone. Now they're dark for everyone. It's a cycle thing, okay?" Roxie held the door open and gestured toward the street. "Would you please leave now? I need to go back to bed."

Karen whimpered and began to prowl the shop far away from the open door. "But I need the information now. I need to know if it will work."

"Please..."

"You have to! You have to tell me if it will work! I know you saw it all, and you just didn't tell me all the rest." The cords stood out on Karen's neck.

"I told you everything I saw. Please leave." Roxie wondered if she was going to have to call the cops to get this nutcase out of her shop.

"No! I saw it in your eyes. I know you saw more. Because you were judging me... I know you were. But I love him! I really love him. We couldn't help it."

"Love who?" Roxie was genuinely mystified.

"Marjorie's husband, George. We didn't mean to fall in love." Karen came closer to Roxanne and then veered away into the herbal section.

"I really think you need to leave now." Roxie left the door to approach the woman, hoping she might be able to herd her out of the store.

"At first, we just joked that we could be together if Marjorie was dead, but at some point, I don't know, we got serious, and we started to think about the best way to kill her." Karen wrung her hands and whimpered again.

A sheet of cold rippled through Roxie's body, and she felt sure the world had shifted six inches to the left. Sure, she thought Marjorie was one of the most annoying women on the planet, but it certainly wasn't worth killing her. Desperate to get Karen out, Roxie's eyes darted around the shop looking for anything that might be helpful in getting a homicidal lunatic to go away. The stock of her store was completely useless to her now. What was she going to do? Light a candle and threaten to singe her arm hair? Then, out of the corner of her eye, she saw it. A faint little glimmer that promised a silver tongue, a bit of speech luck fluttering past the philosophy shelf in the book section. She shot a quick glance at Karen and confirmed she was looking the other way before she lunged for the luck. The silver strip of luck was slippery and thrashed in her fingers like a minnow, but she held on and stuffed it in her mouth. Suddenly, she knew exactly what to say to get Karen to walk out the door.

"I have to know if our plan will work, Roxanne. I don't want to go to jail. It's not our fault... love isn't a crime." Karen turned to face Roxie, her eyes wide and pleading.

"The kind of seeing you need takes time to prepare. This won't just be a quick turn of the cards or glance at your palm. Come after I close the shop at 8:00 tomorrow night. I don't want to take the chance we'll be disturbed." She gestured to the still open door. "I'll even give you a 10% discount if you leave right now."

"Oh thank you, thank you!" Karen cried as she fairly skipped to the door. "You've made me so happy."

Roxie shut the door behind Karen and leaned against it, trembling. She had no idea what she was going to do when she was alone tomorrow night at 8:00 and a woman capable of killing showed up at her door, a killer she invited.

Roxie stood on her roof in the twilight, still contemplating her dilemma. The luck should have still been thick, as it had been the night before, but all she'd managed to catch was a few minor fingerlings of luck, now safely tucked in clear glass test tubes. These bits of luck would hardly be good for anything, but Roxie caught them anyway to stay loose for the larger prey that would hopefully swim in on the darker currents in the deep night hours. A dark patch of bad luck, no bigger than a quarter, wriggled in the corner near the air handler. Normally, she didn't bother with the bad luck. Bad luck could be worse than no luck, and no luck was bad enough. She only bothered to catch the darker stuff when she had a specific reason for it. But there was nothing else to catch at the moment, and she needed to stay limber.

She selected a huge tiger's eye marble and stalked her prey on silent cat feet. As she slapped the marble down and spoke the word of power, she felt an electric tingle run up her arm. Bad luck always bit back. Meandering back to her boxes, Roxie rolled the marble around in her palm and returned back to her previous thoughts. With her trained eye, she could see the little greasy cloud roiling inside. She idly wondered what she would ever use it for. Sniffing the marble, she wrinkled her nose at the rotten egg stench.

Roxie was just about to toss it back in the box when the solution hit her. She reared her head back and inhaled deeply. It was faint, but there. Pacing toward the south end of the building, the smell was stronger. What she needed was definitely out there, but she was going to need some extra tools if she was going to call in that much bad luck and succeed in capturing it. She tucked the marble in her pocket and flew down the stairs to collect what she needed from the back room of the shop.

She was out of breath when she hauled herself up the last few steps back to the roof. Roxie smelled again and found that the huge cloud of bad luck she'd caught wind of was still in range. She took a handful of ashes and flung them skyward, sending thoughts of loneliness with them. The cloud of luck turned and drifted closer. With a shaky breath, she tossed out the used up matches from her pocket and pushed out a wave of bitterness with them. The cloud of foul luck picked up speed, and Roxie could feel a hot psychic wind in her face. For the final call, she called up the saddest memory of her life, the day her mother finally gave up her battle with breast cancer, and forced the tears to roll down her face.

A thick black cloud rushed and swirled right over her head. Roxie shoved her hands into the thick leather electrician's gloves an old boyfriend had left behind and pulled a menacing red witch ball from the box of clean containers. She raised it above her head with both hands and cried out the word of power into the roaring psychic wind. The bad luck screamed into the witch ball, and the electricity jolting down her arms knocked her flat, in spite of the heavy leather gloves. But she managed not to drop the witch ball on her way down. Sitting up, she looked at the delicate ball in her hands and watched the malevolent glow pulse against the backdrop of leather scorched black.

As Roxie suspected, Karen was early and fidgety. At 7:30, she pretended to be interested in books on dowsing while Roxie helped a local witch pick out a new pendulum. At 7:45, she gave the basket of rose quartz crystals a desultory paw while Roxie wrapped up some Dragon's Blood incense for a tattooed Goth boy. At 7:53, she set Roxie's nerves on edge by tinking the wind chimes with her fingernail while she stared daggers at the shop clock, and Roxie measured out dried marigold petals for the sweet lady who lived down the street. Karen nearly squealed in excitement when Roxie showed the last customer out at 8:07 and locked the door behind him.

"Now? You'll tell me what I need to know now?" Karen's words came all out in a rush.

Roxie nodded. "This way." And she led Karen to the counter. She dug for the box underneath and drew out the red glass witch ball. Just looking at it made her queasy.

Karen sucked in her breath. "It's beautiful." Roxie handed it to her without a word. Karen cooed and gasped while she admired the trinket in her hands. "What do we do with it?"

"Come with me," said Roxie. "We need to do this kind of reading in the back where there's more floor space."

Karen stepped away from the counter and started to head for wands, when Roxie let her hand slip casually in her pocket and just as casually draw out the tiger's eye marble. She stepped past Karen and let the marble slip out of numb fingers. Karen stepped on the marble and pitched forward, and she smashed the witch ball between the floor and her chest, right over her heart. Roxie watched the greasy, black luck soak into Karen like a sponge.

"What did you do? What did you do?" Roxie screeched at Karen.

"It was an accident, I swear! Just bad luck..." Karen stuttered.

"Get out! Just get out!" Roxie pointed imperiously to the door. "I can't have your foul the energy in here."

"But, but..." Karen climbed to her feet, offering her hands, covered in shallow cuts from the broken glass.

"Leave now." Roxie put all her anger and disgust into her voice.

Karen fled, weeping. Roxie shut her eyes. She heard the squeal of brakes out in the street and the sickening sound of metal meeting flesh. Then, she locked the door and turned out the lights, turning her back on the gabble of voices in the street.

# Kissed by a Fairy

It was her tears that drew the fairies to her as she sobbed in the lee of the stone wall in the back garden of her parent's Ruxton rancher just off Bellona Avenue. Most humans don't realize how fascinated fairies are with tears. The Unseelie folk are enthralled with how easily humans cry, and they are also a little bit jealous. Even in depths of misery, fairies are rarely granted the comfort of tears. But then there is also the salt - fairies hunger for salt.

Christine's round tears were full of salt as they coursed down her face, and the fairies gathered, unnoticed, around her. At first, there were two, then three, then half a dozen, all waiting for the distraught blonde girl to notice them. Finally, Aeryn, Mistress of the Queen's Wardrobe, cleared her throat loudly.

Christine started and looked all around. She did not see the fairies at first, but then her eyes adjusted to the magic as eyes might adjust to the sun when one steps out into a bright day from the dimness of an office. Her eyes goggled at the diminutive woman in front of her. The top of Aeryn's head barely met her breastbone. Aeryn cocked her head to the side, her waist-length brown hair swaying. The pink of her long dress mimicked her round pink cheeks, and her glimmering green eyes put Christine to mind of dragon flies.

"Who the hell are you?" Christine demanded as she knuckled the tears out of her eyes.

"That's really no way to greet your savior, now is it?" Aeryn's voice tinkled like little silver bells rung by raindrops.

"Savior? Who says I need a savior?" she said, wiping her nose on her baggy sweatshirt sleeve.

"Perhaps you don't," Aeryn allowed. "But then, why are you crying alone in the garden?"

"That's none of your business." Christine drew herself up and did her best to look down her nose at the growing throng of fairies that stared at her with unabashed curiosity.

"Perhaps if you made it my business we could assist one another." Aeryn rocked on her heels and folded her hands in front of her.

"What can you do for me?"

"I might be able to do something about that child growing in your belly."

Christine sucked her breath in through her teeth. "How do you know about that? I haven't told anyone. I just found out myself!" She glanced back at the house, hoping no one had noticed her voice rising in hysteria.

"We fairies are good at smelling things. And you smell with child. It smells like springtime when the earth is wet and new and growing. Delicious." Aeryn's eyes closed halfway as a look of bliss overtook her face.

"Fairies? You must be joking, right?" Christine craned her head around looking for her friends. "This is a practical joke. Did Amy put you up to this?" She laughed nervously.

"Is this a practical joke?" Aeryn nodded to the rest, and as one, they unfurled their diaphanous water color wings and began to hover and flit around the garden.

"Hey! Stop that!" Christine hissed as she motioned for them to settle down. "Someone might see you."

Aeryn alighted on a spot in front of Christine. "No one will see us unless we wish them to. But anyone can see you windmilling your arms around like an idiot."

Christine tucked her hands into her armpits.

"Now, can we talk like civilized creatures?"

"Ok," said Christine. "But I really don't see what you can do for me."

"I propose an exchange. You have something we need, and you want something we can do."

"You wanna fill me in on your logic since I seem to be missing a beat?"

"We need the baby you carry inside of you. Fairy blood is notoriously thin, and now and then, a touch of human blood in the line helps us along."

"I'm not giving you my baby!" Christine's hands flew to her still flat belly.

"Why not?" Aeryn looked genuinely puzzled. "You don't want it for yourself, do you?"

"Well, no… I'm only sixteen. Having a baby right now would ruin my life. Not to mention my parents would kill me."

"So, why not give us the baby?"

"I don't even want to have it. Can you just imagine what my friends would say if I was parading around with this huge belly? And then there's the 'rents. You can't forget how they're going to kill me if they know I'm pregnant."

"And here is where the bargain comes in." Aeryn smiled wide. "We fairies can fix it so no one will ever know that you are with child. Not your parents, not your teachers, not even the young man who planted the seed."

"You can actually do that?" Christine looked skeptical.

"No one sees us unless we want them to. We can easily throw the same glamour over you."

"Ok, so that's the deal? You make sure no one ever knows I'm pregnant, and I give you the baby when I have it?"

"Yes, Mistress, you seem to have grasped the essentials of the offer."

"I don't know. I could always go to Planned Parenthood. I mean, what else am I going to get out of this?"

"We can make sure the birthing doesn't hurt. We'll take you over to Fairie and use a spell so you won't feel any pain. And you'll be tended by the Queen's Ladies themselves."

"I guess… oh, I don't know." Christine shifted from one foot to another.

"Well, the queen herself did authorize me to give one more thing to sweeten the pot if you balked."

"And?"

"If you give the queen a daughter, she will grant you a favor of your own choosing at any time in the future."

"A favor? That's it?" Christine raised her eyebrow.

Aeryn's jaw dropped open. "Do you have any idea how valuable an unnamed favor from a fairy is? And from the Queen of the Fairies, no less? You could parlay that into nearly anything."

"Anything?" Christine rubbed her chin.

"Yes, anything!"

"No one will ever know I'm pregnant, and if I give her a girl, she'll give me a favor worth almost anything?"

"Yes." Aeryn twisted her hands together.

Christine paused for one more moment. "You've got a deal."

Aeryn's shoulders relaxed and a grin lit up her face. "You won't regret this, Christine. You will have the eternal gratitude of the Fairy people." She dug about in the folds of her gown and produced a vial, no bigger than the smallest finger on a human hand, made of the finest crystal and stoppered with virgin beeswax, filled with a swirling, glowing pink liquid. She held it out.

"Drink this."

"Wait a minute," Christine said as she accepted the bottle. "I kinda remember something from the fairytale unit in English. Isn't there something about you guys being able to trap me if I eat or drink anything you give me?"

"That only applies when you are within the borders of Fairie." Aeryn sighed. "Now, drink up. That's the only way we can get the spell to work."

Christine worked out the stopper and saluted the fairies with the vial. "Bottoms up," she said and tossed back the contents quickly. She waited for a moment with a confused look on her face.

"I don't feel any different." She handed the empty vial back to Aeryn.

"Trust me," said Aeryn. "It's working already. No one will know about your condition but us. I'll be sending others with additional draughts of the potion when they are necessary. Thank you, Christine."

And with that, the fairies faded back into the garden and left Christine to wonder just what exactly she had done.

When the moon was full again, Christine found another fairy, smaller than Aeryn, flittering at her bedroom window with another vial of potion. She drank it down, and when she handed the vial back to the fairy, she said, "I don't think this is working right. Could you send Aeryn by?"

The fairy bowed and disappeared. Not long after, as she struggled with her geometry homework, there was another knock at the window. Aeryn hovered there. Christine motioned her inside, and in spite of the fairy's reassurance that no one could see her unless she wanted them to, Christine looked over the neighborhood to make sure no one had seen before she shut the window.

"I hope you're not planning on reneging on our deal." Aeryn planted her fists on her hips.

"Not as long as it works," Christine said. She yanked up her shirt to expose her slightly swelling belly. "Look, I'm showing."

"Of course you can see it." Aeryn rolled her eyes. "You know the truth, and a glamour spell doesn't work on someone who knows the truth."

"Oh, well excuse me for not knowing the rules of magic." Christine rolled her eyes. "But how do I know for sure?"

"You could try it out." Aeryn shrugged. "Don't you humans have some sort of mass bathing ritual after group physical activity?"

"Do you mean gym?" Christine giggled. "I wouldn't exactly call it a ritual. But I suppose I could try it tomorrow. We do have volleyball."

"As you wish." Aeryn bowed. "Is there anything else I can do for you?"

"I guess, umm... well, there is this one thing." Christine blushed.

"Yes?"

"Can you tell me if the baby is alright? I mean, I'm not going to the doctor and all, and then there's all this magic stuff. I guess I'm just a little worried."

Aeryn stepped forward and laid her hands against Christine's ever-so-slightly swelling belly. She frowned, her brow furrowed, and moved her hands to a different position.

"What's wrong?" Christine's voice cracked.

"Nothing," Aeryn murmured and shifted her hands again. "The baby is just fine, as far as I can tell. I'm just not getting as clear a read as I do with fairy women. It must be because you're human."

"Oh," said Christine. "Do you think I should go to the doctor just to be sure?"

"Not unless you want the glamour to fall apart," said Aeryn. "Remember, if anyone knows the truth, the glamour won't fool them."

"Oh, I don't want that to happen. That would just screw everything up."

"Yes, it would," Aeryn said mildly. "Is there anything else you need?"

"Not unless you know anything about geometry."

Aeryn pulled a face. "The human sciences never were my forte." She patted Christine's hand. "Everything will be just fine, my dear."

"Thanks," said Christine as she let Aeryn out the window.

The next day after volleyball, Christine hung toward the back of the pack of girls swarming into the locker room. These girls had all know each other since their earliest memories and the expensive private preschools their parents had fought tooth and nail to get them into. As soon as they were out of the line of sight of the door, they were all shedding their sweaty t-shirts and shorts and flinging their still-tied running shoes into their lockers with resounding thuds. Christine hesitated one more moment, then took a deep breath and began shedding her own clothes. She could hear the water hissing on behind her, and all of her friends giggling and splashing each other.

She stepped into the shower area, hoping no one would notice how badly she was shaking or that she was four months pregnant and obviously showing to anyone not under the influence of fairies.

"Hey, Christine," called her best friend Amy. "What's different? There's something different about you."

"I don't know what you're talking about." Christine felt herself turn bright red and nearly turned on her heel to run out of the shower area.

"I know," crowed Amy. "You've lost weight! Your stomach is so flat. I'm totally jealous. What's your secret? C'mon, spill."

Christine heaved a great sigh of relief as she stepped under the water.

"Just the extra crunches, I guess. No big deal."

It took Christine a little while to get used to the bowing fairies. Everywhere she went, there they were: perching on tree limbs, peeking out from under bushes, emerging from the blossoms of flowers in every garden she passed. They stared at her in wonderment and bowed low. They left her gifts of shells, feathers, and pretty stones, sometimes even fruit.

"They have to stop!" She wailed to Aeryn. "People are noticing that weird things happen to me. It's embarrassing!"

"Christine," Aeryn soothed. "The Fairie people are just overjoyed to see a new member of the royal family on the way. It hasn't happened in nearly two centuries."

"But it's embarrassing!"

"You have to allow them some outlet. I can't just make them stop all together." Aeryn said, exasperated.

"Can they just do it around my house?" Christine whined. "Maybe try to only do it where my parents won't notice?"

"We will try to contain our excitement. But don't worry, it won't be long now." And Aeryn stroked Christine's burgeoning belly.

As the students stepped off the bus, the humid air of oncoming summer in the Nation's capital wrapped around them like sodden wool blankets. Christine shifted from foot to foot, even more miserable than most because of her full term belly that no one else could see.

"Tell me again why this fieldtrip is supposed to be a good idea?" Amy muttered to her.

"Visiting downtown D.C. is good for our moral character." Christine sighed. "Something about the seat of law blah, blah, blah and lots of other boring stuff."

"Oh, right." Amy wiped the sweat off her forehead and stared off into space.

Christine spotted the first fairy face of the day peering out from under a rhododendron leaf at the botanical garden. She saw him immediately and, with the ease of long practice, didn't let any surprise show on her face. In the months since she had struck her deal, it had gotten easier and easier to spot the fairies. She learned to distinguish between types and even spot fairy cousins, like leprechauns or brownies, that weren't quite fairies but were still interested in the coming addition to the royal line. Contrary to most human belief, fairies weren't all alike. Some were human-sized and tall and willowy. Others were so small as to perch easily in the palm of Christine's hand. Some had wings, while others didn't.

The fairy hiding under the rhododendron was one of the smaller, wingless types. When he stood tall, he might come to a human's knee. He wore bright blue clothes and a jaunty red cap over his pointed features. He gestured urgently to Christine. She drifted away from the group casually until she was near enough to hear the fairy.

"You're not supposed to be here," she hissed.

"Mistress," he said in his high, reedy voice. "You must come with me."

"Why?" Christine craned her head to see if anyone was looking.

"It is time."

"Time for what?" She pretended to be interested in the plaque that described the normal habitat of the rhododendron.

"The child." His voice betrayed his impatience. "Your pains will soon be on you, and we must have you to Fairie before they start."

"I can't just leave now," she protested. "If I leave the fieldtrip, I'll be in so much trouble with my parents. Everyone will notice and ask why."

"I have no concern for how your humans will react. My concern is for the child."

"Well, I care how my humans will react. I have to live with them for the rest of my life. That's the whole reason I struck the deal for the glamour in the first place."

The fairy sighed and rubbed his temples. "When can you get away?"

"We're supposed to be home by five o'clock. Meet me in my bedroom." She motioned him away with her hands as the rest of the bored teenagers came to join her with their equally bored guide as he explained all about rhododendrons.

Christine's first pains came among the roses in the early afternoon part of the tour, right after lunch. Her face creased in pain, and a small cry escaped her lips.

"What's wrong, Chris?" Amy laid a gentle hand on her shoulder.

"Umm… stomach cramp. I don't think lunch agreed with me."

"Yeah, that cafeteria sucked. Do you want me to see if I can get some Pepto from Mr. Briggs?"

"No, I should be okay until I get home." Secretly, Christine hoped she wasn't lying.

Christine's lips were sore from biting them by the time she waddled through her bedroom door. Aeryn had nearly worn a hole in the carpet from pacing. She flew at Christine and grabbed both of her arms, hard.

"Where have you been?" she hissed.

"Oww, Aeryn! I couldn't get away. I can't raise suspicion."

"You should have risked it." Aeryn's grip tightened. "You have jeopardized the heir."

Christine looked into Aeryn's eyes and gasped at the fire she saw there. "I thought you were my friend," she whimpered. "Why are you yelling at me? I'm trying to do everything right... really I am."

Aeryn loosened her grip and unclenched her jaw. "I'm sorry. But you've given us quite a fright. The child must be born within the borders of Fairie." Aeryn's voice was tight and stiff. "Here, drink this." She thrust another crystal vial into the girl's hands, the glowing, swirly liquid in this one was green instead of the usual pink. Christine threw it back with ease of practice but never took her wary eyes off the fairy.

Aeryn turned to a blank bit of wall and surveyed it for a moment. She gave a short nod and fished what looked like an ordinary piece of chalk from her girdle. Starting at the peak and with two great arcing lines, she traced the rough outline of a doorway. Instead of leaving ghostly white marks against the pink paint, the chalk left behind lines that glowed and writhed with all the colors of the rainbow. On the right side of the doorway, she drew a complicated glyph that seemed to dance from the color and light. She drew its sister glyph on the left, not quite the same but close enough to be mistaken for one another if you didn't look closely. As the glyphs danced and twirled in place, Aeryn stood on her tip toes and outlined a key stone at the peak of the door. She dropped back to her heels for a moment and shook her drawing hand out. Then, she took a deep breath and, with a wrinkled brow, returned to her toes and began to draw a new completely different glyph in the keystone.

This glyph glowed like the others but the light was darker, not quite malevolent but definitely not cheerful. While door side glyphs were built of graceful loops and whorls, this glyph was hard edges and angles. Aeryn finished and rocked back on her heels. She wiped the sweat from her brow. Christine opened her mouth to ask a question, but before she could wrap her mouth around it another contraction clutched her belly, and she let out a moan. Aeryn held out her hand toward Christine.

"Take my hand now. We don't have much time."

Slightly hunched over from the pain, she took Aeryn's hand as she returned the chalk to her girdle. Panting and weak, Christine leaned again the fairy woman, her former wariness temporarily forgotten. Aeryn spared only one glance down at her suffering charge as she raised her free hand and began to speak.

The words made Christine forget the pain in her back and belly. The words skipped and leapt and wreathed around each other as Aeryn chanted in a language that shimmered brightly like handfuls of fresh gold and copper and silver. Christine felt the words slide down her skin, silken and soft, cocooning her in a comfort she'd never known. The words were familiar and foreign all at once. The girl thought she could understand them if she could just focus enough, but even as she thought it, she was distracted by the sheer joy the unknown words placed in her heart.

So when the chalk lines on her bedroom wall began to bloom stones, Christine only smiled. Rough gray stones rounded and popped out of her bedroom wall, forming the frame of the door while the paint surrounded by the stones shimmered and rippled and resolved itself into a rough hewn oak door bound by metal hinges. Aeryn supported Christine to the door and rapped sharply three times. The heavy door swung impossibly inward and revealed a stooped granny fairy on the other side. Behind her was a huge bedroom that would have been at home in any ancient European castle.

"It took ye long enough," said the granny. "I was about to send the seneschals out after ye."

"Enough, you old crone," huffed Aeryn. "Just take her. She's already pretty far gone." She handed her charge over the threshold.

Christine felt her body quiver and shift somehow otherly. The granny wrapped her bony arms around her. Though the crone's arms appeared frail as willow branches, they held her with the strength of an oak.

"Oh dear," Christine said, clutching her stomach.

"Bucket!" shouted the granny over her shoulder.

A sweet lavender fairy lady in waiting got the bucket under Christine just in time for her to empty her stomach.

"I'm sorry, I'm sorry." Christine sobbed as she retched over and over.

"Don't worry, sweeting," the granny said as she stroked Christine's back. "Every human gets ill when they cross over, and the babe in your belly makes it doubly hard for you. Why, you're doing better than some the big strapping knights I've seen wander through. Cloth." She accepted a cool damp cloth from faceless hands and mopped Christine's sweaty brow and then wiped her mouth with firm and gentle strokes born of long practice.

"Are ye done now?"

"I think so."

"Alright then. Let's get her into bed then and see what we can do about giving our queen an heir."

Christine felt at least a dozen hands support her as she drifted to the opulent bed hung with pale blue velvet curtains, her feet barely touching the floor. Willing hands cradled her and lifted her into the lush feather bed. She relaxed back into the cloud like softness as nimble fingers plucked and tugged at the buttons and zippers of her clothing. In moments, she found herself naked. The granny leaned in close and traced the five moles on Christine's sternum, just between her breasts.

"The Fairy star," she said with wonder. "No wonder Aeryn cold smell you so well. You've got blood of the Unseelie folk somewhere back in your family."

Christine tried to sit up and squawk a protest but the nimble fingers were back, sweeping a voluminous nightgown of fine unbleached linen over her head. While she was still sitting up, the lavender fairy took a position behind her and clucked at dismay at the long braids in her hair.

"'Tis bad luck to have knots around a birthing babe," she said and undid the braids with swift fingers and combed out Christine's fine blonde hair into a shimmering wave of pale silk down her back. The girl tried to say thank you but another contraction rippled through her belly.

"Ease her back, ladies," the granny said. "Time to check her progress."

Christine lay back gasping in pain as the granny checked between her knees. "Little over half way done," she announced to the room, and the fairy ladies laughed and clapped with glee.

"Why does it still hurt? Aeryn promised it wouldn't hurt."

"Well, ya waited a bit long to come to us, dearie. I'll see what I can do, but even magic has its limits."

The granny shuffled off to the corner of the room, and Christine could hear tinkles and clicks over the susurrus murmur of fairy voices. The granny came to where she lay on her back with a stone in each hand. In her right was an opaque, irregular lump of glowing white crystal, and in her left was a smooth, black stone that seemed to suck in all the light.

"It's the best I can do on short notice," she said as she laid the white crystal on Christine's belly and murmured a few sharp fairy words, then laid the smooth stone on Christine's forehead and murmured soft fairy words that came falling out of her mouth like smooth, river-worn pebbles. She felt the ease from the fairy words, again feeling like she could understand if she could just concentrate but not quite being able to. The white stone filled her belly with warmth, and the black stone sent soothing waves of cool down her forehead. The next contraction came, and there was pain, but Christine felt one step away from it. She knew her body clutched and ached and pushed and trembled and sweated, but it did not touch her.

And so it continued for hours. There was sweat and, inevitably, blood. Christine remained in her detached fog and barely blinked as she noticed some of the fairy women collect her birthing blood in vials and spirit it away. She wondered what they would use it for but could not seem to rouse the energy to care. And then, eventually, in those strange hours that are neither night nor morning, the child was born.

"A girl! A girl!" the cry went up, and even in her muzzy state, Christine thought she could hear bells pealing. She heard the baby cry and searched her heart for that stirring of emotion that every mother is supposed to have but found her heart surprisingly blank. It was just another baby crying, and she wished someone would shut it up. It was a relief when the Royal Nanny removed the newborn princess from the birthing chamber to the queen's apartments so that the squalling child could be inspected by her adoptive mother.

A smaller cadre of women stayed to care for Christine in her after pains. When all was finally done and the granny was satisfied that Christine was finished laboring and ready to go home, the stones were removed. Christine felt twinges of pain and swirls of emotion but fought to retain the serene, unbothered state. The faceless hands came about her again. The gown was removed, and her body washed. Her hair was braided, and she was dressed in her own clothes again. The granny handed her yet another potion, this one a swirling rainbow, and urged her to drink.

"This will put your body back right."

Christine tossed it back without question, and she was lead back to the portal. Just as she was about to cross, a bright silver coin was pressed into her palm by unknown hands.

"When you need your favor, use this," whispered a voice in her ear.

She felt the otherly shift again as she passed the threshold and felt profoundly relieved that she didn't get sick again on her own side. None of the fairy women crossed with her. They all fidgeted in the doorway and seemed eager to get away.

"Thank you, Christine," said the old granny. "You've done us a great service today. We will not forget you."

And the door swung shut and faded until it was nothing more than a smooth, pink bedroom wall again. She looked around her familiar room. For all the time she felt she had been gone, the clock only showed two hours passed. Christine looked down at the coin in her hand. It nearly glowed with silvery light. On one side was a spreading oak tree and on the other was the profile of an ethereal lady. She tucked the coin into the bottom of her jewelry box, under the costume jewelry she'd worn for homecoming.

Christine undressed, sat on the edge of her bed, and took a physical inventory. Indeed, everything was back where it had been from before the baby. In fact, everything was intact. Not even her doctor would be able to tell she'd had sex. After she changed into her nightgown and slid under the covers, she searched her heart again and again found it blank.

As time passed, Christine found that the memories of her time as a surrogate mother for the Fairy Queen faded. She graduated high school with honors and with her father's connections attended a prestigious East coast university. She did well, but not spectacularly, and decided on a career in public relations. Her parents were pleased when she finished her MBA and steadily made her way up the corporate ladder. She met a nice young man, an assistant to the Mayor of Baltimore, when he was looking for help from her firm. They carried on a long courtship and eventually moved in together. Christine's parents were not overjoyed with this development even though they liked the young man very well, but they trusted their daughter's judgment. After all, she'd always been so sensible and never done drugs or gotten into trouble like the children of some of their friends. After living together for five years, the young man proposed to her during an afternoon picnic in Druid Hill Park. Her parents were thrilled to throw their only daughter a lavish wedding. It only took her mother a month to start asking when the grandchildren would be coming.

Christine and her husband did start trying for children almost immediately. They tried for a year with no results, all the while telling their families that they were not ready to try for children yet. They wanted their children to be a surprise. Then, sick of enduring the questions from their over eager parents, she and her husband did tell them they were trying. After six months, her mother began to send her emails and pamphlets about infertility. Christine was starting to head into the danger zone at the age of 37. It was then that Christine thought of the girl child she'd left in Fairie for the first time in almost 20 years. She wondered if that was the only child her body would ever grant her. She didn't tell her husband about these private fears. He had believed her when she said she lost her virginity to her college sweetheart after homecoming her freshman year.

Another six months passed, and Christine found herself consulting fertility doctors. She counted her lucky stars that she lived in the Baltimore/D.C. metro area, home to many of the top specialists. The doctors assured the couple that theirs was not an unusual case. Many couples were waiting longer to have children for a variety of reasons. A few simple rounds of basic IVF should provide them with the child they dreamed of. The nurse smiled when she took Christine's blood for routine tests and said that it might even take on the first try.

Christine and her husband went home with appointments for egg and sperm harvesting in their day planners and congratulated themselves on how sensibly they were handling such an emotional situation. That night, while her husband was on the phone, Christine went through her jewelry box. Wedged in the back corner of a little used drawer was a tiny black velvet bundle. She unwrapped the silver coin she had received so many years ago for her service to the Fairy Queen. The weight of the coin was familiar in her hand as she remembered watching the doorway to the fairy realm disappear from her bedroom wall. She remembered snipping a small bit of velvet to wrap it in from the inside hem of her junior prom dress just before she gave the dress away to charity. The coin still shined with ethereal light, unchanged from the day it had been pressed into her palm. She turned it over and over in her hand and wondered if the Fairy Queen would have any power over pregnancy in the human realm. She heard the light step of her husband behind her and quickly wrapped the coin and returned it to its place.

"Whatcha doin', hon?" He entered, loosening his tie.

"Just taking a walk down memory lane. Looking at some of my old junk." Christine forced a laugh. "You ready for bed?"

"You bet," he said as he wrapped his around her waist and laid a theatrically sloppy kiss on her cheek. "Hell, maybe we'll make a baby without any help tonight."

Christine laughed for real this time and was happy to be led to bed.

It was summer again, and Christine was in the final stages of pregnancy. She waddled around her own back garden huffing in the stifling, humid August air. Why do I always finish in the summer? she wondered to herself. Looking at the house, she considered going back into the air conditioning but then thought of how claustrophobic the walls of her own home were. She just couldn't seem to stay still, just as it had been with the first child when she was 16. Christine thought of all the silent comparisons she had made these past eight months, unable to share them because no one in the mortal realm knew of her first birth. She had cried over the news of both pregnancies; the first from fear and anger and the second from joy that a round of IVF had finally taken. This time around, she'd had morning sickness morning, noon, and night when she'd never had a moment of nausea the first time around. Christine wondered if it was from the potion or if it was just the difference between a 39-year-old body and a 16-year-old body. She was getting just as big, though. The first time she had looked like she had a watermelon under her skin, and her belly looked just the same this time, only this time other people could see it too.

It was the shifting leaves of a low azalea bush that caught her eye. The air was still, and there was not a single breeze to rifle them, yet the leaves shimmied just a bit. Studying the bush closely, she saw there was a little fairy man in blue clothes and a red cap, perhaps even the same little man who came to her in the gardens so long ago. She glanced around herself to make sure she was alone.

"Hello?" she said softly, bending down as far as her belly would let her to get a better look at him.

"Oh good," he said. "You can see me still. I thought your Sight might be a little rusty after all this time."

"Thank you," said Christine. "I think. But what are you doing here? I haven't had any dealings with fairies in years."

"I know, dearie. But I was just in the neighborhood, and I could smell that you're just about to pop, and I thought I'd do the neighborly thing and let you know."

"You mean it's time?" Her hand dropped to her belly.

"You have a few hours yet before the pains set in," he said. "But you humans do seem to have trouble moving around quickly - never understand why you just don't use magic - and I thought you might want to call that husband of yours."

"Thank you very much. Is there anything I can do for you?"

"Oh no, my lady. I'm still repaying you for bringing us our princess. She's quite a gem she is, our Leaitha. I think she'll be one of the finest queens our realm has seen. But I must be going." And the little man was gone as suddenly as he had come. As Christine straightened, she felt an odd twinge in her heart. She stood squinting in the sun, trying to decide if her labor pains were coming on faster than the fairy had thought but then realized that it was pride in her heart.

Christine wandered back into the house bewildered and called her husband in a daze. She told him she knew she was being silly but that her hormones were running wild and she needed him home right away to massage her aching feet and bring a pint of triple chocolate chunk ice cream please. The fairy man was right, and by the time her husband made it home through rush hour traffic, she was in labor, and they headed to hospital.

It was a boy, hale and hearty. He had his mother's liquid brown eyes and his father's round cheeks. He was the treasure of his parents' hearts. The labor was reasonably easy for a mother of Christine's age, and it wasn't long before Liam's parents were tucking him into his crib at home.

"Did you check on Liam?" Christine slid into bed beside her sleepy husband.

"Yup." He let out a great yawn. "He's fine. I even watched him breathe for a while. You better get some sleep before he wakes up for another feeding."

Despite her husband's advice, Christine could not sleep. She tossed and turned and punched her pillow. Her husband's rhythmic breathing usually soothed her, but not this time. When she could not stand staring at the ceiling any longer, she slipped out of bed to go watch her son sleep.

Christine eased herself into the rocking chair in the nursery, her body still aching from the birth in deep places. Not for the first time, she wished for another vial of the fairy potion that had set her body right before. She settled into the soft cushions of the chair with a sigh and cast her eyes to the crib and smiled. The smile slowly melted off her face.

Something was wrong with Liam. His body was too stiff. His breathing was just not right. Christine knew her son's breathing well enough after watching him for a few weeks to know that something was horribly wrong. Leaping from her chair, she stumbled a bit as the rocker slapped the backs of her calves. She tore back the blanket, and her vision blurred. From one eye, it seemed she could see her son fast asleep, dreaming peacefully, while from the other eye she saw a pile of twigs and leaves animated by magic to imitate the movement of breathing. She rubbed her eyes with the heels of her hands and looked down again. Sticks and twigs.

"Fairies," she spat and made for her own bedroom. Christine moved quickly but as quietly as possible, ignoring the protests from her aching body. Tearing through her jewelry box, she found the silver coin she sought. She glanced over her shoulder to make sure that her husband was still sleeping and when she saw that he was, she stole barefoot into the back garden.

Standing in a pool of moonlight in the middle of the patio, the frigid flagstones sent waves of cold up through her feet. Her heart thumped hard, and she could feel the edges of the coin biting into her palm. Her mouth hung open on a cry she did not know how to form. How did one call the Fairy Queen? She knew what she wanted but was at a loss for how to make it happen. The fairies had always come to her without any effort on her part before.

The night breeze blew her nightgown around her, molding it to her body, and she looked down at the coin in her hand with tendrils of hair blowing across her face. The coin absorbed the moonlight and began to glow brighter in her hand. She looked more closely and saw the tree stamped into the coin swaying in a breeze, the sound of soft rustling coming up from her palm. She flipped the coin over and saw that the woman's head blink.

"Can you hear me?" Christine whispered to the coin in her hand.

The woman's face turned to her, from profile to full face and said in a cold, imperious voice, "What do you want?"

"I need to see you. You owe me a favor." Christine's voice shook.

"Very well." The coin sighed.

The glow in her palm grew brighter and stronger until she had to turn her head away and shield her eyes with her other hand. She could feel the coin in her hand grow warmer and tremble a bit. Then the warmth was gone, and the coin was still.

"Well, what do you want?" said the same imperious voice, but louder this time. "I haven't got all night."

Christine lowered her hand and looked around to find the coin had turned to a simple coin in her hand, plain silver with no glow, and in front of her stood a fairy woman of ethereal, icy beauty clad in silver and pale blue. Christine was so stunned by her beauty that it took her a moment to find her voice.

"My son," she croaked.

"Pardon me?" The Fairy Queen examined the hem of her sleeve in studied boredom.

"You're the Fairy Queen, yes?" Christine drew herself up a bit taller.

"Of course I am." The Queen looked down her nose.

"You must grant me a favor for my service, right?" Christine brought the coin close to her chest.

"I never renege on my word." The Queen's chin lifted.

"My son, Liam, is gone. And there's a pile of breathing twigs and leaves in his crib - it's a changeling. I know you took him! I promised you one of my children, not all of them." Christine's voice was beginning to rise.

"Calm yourself, Mistress," said the Queen.

"I will calm myself when I am holding my son in my arms again." The words left Christine in a hiss.

"State your favor clearly, Mistress." The frost in the Queen's voice would have made a polar bear shiver.

"I want you to bring my son, Liam, home to me, and I want him home tonight, and I want him home the same age as when he left." Christine lifted her chin defiantly.

"Anything else?" The Queen's eyebrows quirked up and she let a small mocking smile dance on her lips.

Christine licked her lips. "I want you to swear that you and your people will never take any of my children, or their children, again."

The Queen nodded. "Well stated, Mistress. You have used your favor wisely. Neither I nor my people will ever take another of your children or their children." She gathered up her skirts and turned to retreat into the depths of the garden.

"Liam?" Christine's voice came out pale and trembling.

"He will be returned to you within the hour by one of my people," the Queen called over her shoulder. "I suggest you wait for him in the nursery." With that, the Fairy Queen vanished from sight.

Christine stood frozen on the patio for only a moment before she raced back inside to the nursery. She didn't want to miss Liam's return. She waited and paced, waited and paced, listening to her husband snore down the hall. Nearly an hour had passed when she saw one of the nursery walls bend and shimmer and heard the light step of a fairy foot on the carpet.

The fairy woman in front of her was, of course, lovely, dressed in sea-foam green with golden blonde hair streaming down her back to her waist. But Christine only had eyes for the lamb's wool wrapped bundle in the fairy's arms. A small, animal cry flew from Christine's lips, and she started forward with her arms outstretched. The fairy woman laid Liam in her arms, and Christine peeled back the blanket. Two eyes, one nose, one mouth, ten fingers, ten toes - and sleeping peacefully. Christine swayed back and forth with her babe in her arms, crooning a wordless tune. With slow, dreamy steps she walked back to the crib but stood rocking and holding her son, loathe to let him out of her arms. But finally she laid him down in his crib and leaned back. She continued to stand, leaning on the edge of the crib, her hand hovering over her son.

"You love him very much, don't you?"

Christine started up and looked behind her. She was surprised to still see the fairy woman there. This time, she actually took in the woman's features, and although she was sure she'd never met her, she could not escape the feeling she should know her. There was something familiar about the shape of her brow and the curve of her chin, like someone she had known once. But it was the eyes that made her gasp, liquid brown eyes. Christine had never seen a fairy with brown eyes. Her hands flew to her mouth.

"He's my brother, isn't he?"

Christine could only nod dumbly as she looked at the child she had given away so many years ago, now grown into a lovely young woman. Leaitha joined Christine at the side of the crib and watched her little brother with her head tilted to one side.

"Why did your people take him? I thought I was only supposed to give them you." Christine watched Liam breathe for several minutes.

Leaitha shrugged. "He smells a little like me, so one of the smaller cousins thought he belonged to me and I had misplaced him."

"Oh," Christine said, and they both fell silent again. The moonbeams shifted across the nursery floor while the women continued to watch the baby.

Leaitha broke the silence this time. "Do you think you would have loved me like you love him if you had kept me?" Her gaze rested on her mother without pity or emotion, just naked curiosity.

Christine started to speak, then stopped. "I don't know," she said finally. "I was so young. I wasn't ready to be a mother, and I probably would have wound up resenting you. I'm ready for Liam. And I wanted him so bad."

"Fair enough. That's an honest answer." Leaitha held Christine's gaze, searching her eyes. Christine looked away first. Both women stood silently watching the baby sleep. Christine was the first to begin crying, but she could not have explained the tears on her face.

"Oh my," Leaitha whispered. "So that's what they feel like." Christine looked up to see a few small tears sliding down her daughter's face. "I've never cried before. I didn't think I could."

Christine nodded and gathered her daughter into her arms, and they held each other and swayed as the tears poured out of them. Then, Leaitha gently pulled away.

"I will protect him, always," she sniffed. "He's my brother, and I will have all of Fairie at my command. He will be the luckiest boy in the world."

"Thank you." Christine smiled.

Leaitha smiled back and leaned forward to kiss her mother on the cheek, and where her lips met her mother's smooth skin, with both of their tears mixing together between, they both felt the tingle of magic. Leaitha leaned back, and they clasped hands between them.

"I should be going. Mother will be expecting me." They hugged one last time, and Leaitha backed slowly away and back to Fairie through the shimmering wall, waving as she went.

Christine's husband found her asleep on the nursery floor in the morning with one arm stretched up to touch Liam in the crib. He laughed as he kissed her forehead and lovingly called her an overprotective mother.

Liam grew up wise and strong and indeed proved to be the luckiest of boys. And his mother never seemed to age, always looking as lovely as she had when Liam was a baby. Her friends always asked her secret, to which she merely laughed and said, "I must have been kissed by a fairy."

# The Gift of a Lifetime

There are some souls that progress in great, long-legged strides through the fabric of the Universe. They leave behind deep footprints of meaning for those who come after to marvel at. And then there are smaller souls, who scamper through on tiny paws, their passage easy to ignore if one is not looking. But the mistake most watchers make is to think these little paw prints make no impression, that they don't make a difference. The truth of the matter is that all sizes of souls can leave a mark on the fabric of the Universe, and sometimes, the smallest of souls can act as a pebble in a pond, rippling outwards and touching more lives than the largest of footprints.

Anca charged across the cobblestones, darting between the wheels of a coach drawn by two bay horses. One hound yelped behind her, and a human cursed about careless dogs. She dodged down an alleyway. There was still one more vicious cur on her trail. She could feel his hot breath on her tail. Why he would feel the need to chase her was a mystery she could not solve. She had only been going through the bins behind the house he and his pack mate shared with the humans. They had some lovely fish bones that the humans wastefully left flesh on, thrown out from earlier in the evening, very fresh. But it seemed that even though they did not want it themselves, the humans wanted to stop anyone else from having it. The man in the house had stood in the doorway, silhouetted against the too bright light, and sent the dogs after her before she could eat enough to fill even a corner of her empty belly.

Anca felt her spirits sink as she skidded to a stop in front of a blank brick wall. The alley was a dead end. She turned to face her tormenter, crouched down, ears back, tail fluffed, hissing and spitting, ready to do battle with a beast four times her size. The German Shepherd flung himself into the air, spittle flying from his jaws, and Anca braced herself for impact.

But it never came.

Anca found herself in a quiet, empty alley across town, but she was not alone. Anca could feel her. All around she felt the warmth and safety of The Great Mother. She did not question her fortune but fell to grooming her disarrayed fur.

The Great Mother allowed her daughter a few moments to regain her composure after the chase. When Anca had at last groomed her fur, carefully nibbled between each toe, and straightened each of her long, lovely whiskers, The Great Mother spoke.

"You are well, child?" She looked at Anca, who sat prim and proper with her tail wrapped neatly around her paws.

"I am well, Mother," Anca said.

"Does this place suit you better than the last?" said The Great Mother.

"Oh yes, Mother," Anca said as she bow-stretched. "You have been most generous to this humble child." The Great Mother's purr filled the alley, and Anca answered with one of her own.

"Would you be willing to undertake a task for me, little one?"

"Of course, Mother." Anca rubbed her face into her forepaws and purred even louder.

"I need you to kill a rat," said The Mother.

Anca sneezed in surprise. "It seems like a very small task, Mother."

"Not all small things are unimportant."

"Yes, Mother." Anca bow-stretched again.

"This rat will kill a human I do not wish to die."

Anca drew back and hissed. "What do I care if a human dies? Humans have never been kind to me."

"This human is important, child." The Mother's voice was gentle yet full of steel.

"Humans throw things at me. They send their dogs to rip me to pieces. And even if I find one to keep me in their home and feed me, they drown my children. They drown your children, Mother!" Anca's voice rose into a yowl of grief.

"There will be a reward, little one," said The Great Mother.

"No reward could be worth helping such cruel creatures," spat Anca.

"Let me show you, child." And The Great Mother touched Anca's mind, and she Saw. She felt gentle fingers in her fur, kind fingers scratched her behind her ears and under her chin. Her belly didn't know hunger, and she knew without a doubt that she would have a safe, warm, and soft place to sleep. She Saw this human who would love and care for her as she herself would care for her own kittens, a human who would never think to harm a whisker on the most helpless of animals, a human who would offer her a lifetime of rest. Anca began to purr again.

"Oh her, yes, Mother, I would save her," Anca said.

"She is not here yet, little one. She is a companion for another lifetime," said The Great Mother.

"Could I have her without killing the rat?"

"I would give her to you if I could, but unless you kill the rat, I cannot."

"But why?" mewled Anca. "Am I not due a lifetime of rest? This one has been so hard."

"Yes, child, you are due, but unless you kill the rat, I cannot give you that particular human," said The Great Mother.

"But why can't I have her?"

"Because unless the rat is killed, it will bite the human and make him sick and die before he can discover the medicine that will save the human you crave so much. Unless he lives, she will die as a child, long before she could care for you."

Anca buried her face in her paws and moaned softly. "I will kill the rat."

As the sun set, The Great Mother led Anca to the back courtyard of the house where she would find the rat. In the gloaming, Anca could hear many rats skittering among the waste pile the humans left behind their home. She smelled them, too, and one of them smelled sour.

"You are doing a great thing," The Great Mother said as she stroked Anca's soul to soothe her. "You will save many lives with what you do tonight."

"There is only one I care about," said Anca, but still she purred.

Darkness seeped further into the courtyard, and the rats grew bolder. Anca could see the fattest and boldest of them perching on top of the trash heap and testing the coming night with their noses.

"Which one?" Anca flexed her forepaws and scraped her claws on the cobblestones.

"Patience, child," said The Great Mother. "Not yet."

Anca hunkered down to wait longer; her mouth was dry. Time passed, and light appeared in the windows of the human house, leaving bright panes of gold on the cooling stones of the yard. The stars came out, one by one, and the bold, fat rats criss-crossed the courtyard on their evening business, and even their shyest brethren perched on the trash heap, testing the night with their noses.

One slow, black rat emerged from the trash heap and began to waddle his way across the yard, seeming to head for the human's home. He was quite nearly as large as Anca herself. His greasy fur was patchy, and the exposed skin was scaly and red, covered with weeping sores. The smell of sickness rolled off him in nauseating waves. Here was the source of the sourness Anca had smelled earlier in the evening.

"That one," The Great Mother breathed into Anca's ear. "That is the one who must die if you are to get your human."

Anca whimpered deep down in her throat, but she thrust aside her fear and focused solely on hunting. She measured her prey and the distance and gathered all of her strength, right down to her bones. She would need it.

The rat was in the center of the courtyard when Anca sprang. Two swift bounds brought her down on top of the rat, and she sank her teeth into the back of his neck. The rat squealed and bucked, but Anca held on with her front claws sunk into his shoulders. The rat tucked his chin in and rolled across the cobbles to dislodge Anca.

Anca rolled off, blood on her claws, and was up on her paws in a flash. She crouched low with her ears flat and tail fluffed and twitching. The rat kept his belly low to the ground as he brought himself around to face Anca. The opponents squared off with narrowed eyes, growling deep in their throats. They circled on another, each looking for a lowered guard or some other bit of luck.

The rat came to the conclusion that Anca was the more determined combatant and began to back away to the garbage heap, hissing as he went. Anca relaxed her body slightly; perhaps this would be easier than she thought. If the rat just left, he would not be able to bite the human, so the human would then not become ill. Perhaps she would not have to risk getting wounded to save the human who would save her human.

"He will come back," The Great Mother whispered in her head. "The rat must die tonight."

Anca launched herself at the rat, and they came together in a mass of snarling fur. Anca locked her teeth into his throat, crushing down on his windpipe. She sank her front claws in his shoulders. The rat squealed and threw himself to the side. This left his soft underside open, and Anca raked his belly with mighty jack rabbit thrusts of her hind legs. The rat twisted and rolled in desperation, squealing all the way, but Anca would not let go. She tightened her jaw down a bit more. Ever more desperate, the rat raked his front claws down Anca's shoulders and sides. But still Anca would not let go. Thrashing in last frantic throes, the rat sank his own teeth into Anca's shoulder. Inside her head, Anca howled in pain and fear, but she did not let go. She tightened her jaw down a bit more.

The rat's struggles grew weaker, his clawing changed to gentle pawing, and then, he was still. Anca drew herself up on her paws and whipped her head back and forth, shaking the limp body of the sick rat, just to be sure. She heard the door of the human dwelling open behind her and a human shouting something, then something hard landed next to her tail.

Anca sprang away from the dead and bloodied rat and landed in a crouch to face her new tormenter. A human female stood silhouetted in the light of the doorway, a fist raised above her head, and shrill curses rolling off her lips. Anca howled and spit at her, ready to continue fighting.

"It is done," The Great Mother whispered. "Run, my child."

Anca ran from the courtyard, away from the screaming human and the bloody rat corpse. She ran and she ran until her paws would carry her no more, and she dropped to her belly, panting, in the quiet shadows of a nameless alley. The poison of the rat's sickness coursed through her body with each beat of her heart. The wounds themselves burned and ached. Anca knew she would die a painful death in this lifetime, she could only hope it would be quick.

"Oh my child, my child," said The Great Mother. "You have done so well, and you have suffered so much."

Anca mewed in her pain and reached for her Mother with her paw. The Great Mother touched her and brought her peace. The Great

Mother eased her from life and released her to the Elsewhere so Anca could rest and prepare to be reborn.

Many lifetimes passed by before Anca was ready to return to life again. Her wounds were deep, and her need for rest was great. But eventually, it was time, and she was reborn, blind and deaf, to a common calico in the home of humans who were neither wealthy nor clever. Anca was not worried. The Great Mother made her a promise, and so Anca was a cheerful kitten while she waited for her human, delighting all who saw her with her gamboling about.

Anca's composure slipped a bit when the not-so-clever humans gave her to a man who smelled of sour smoke and spoiled food. The man took her to his home and gave her to a brittle woman who slept too much and ate too little. They fought often, screaming at each other and flinging things. Anca learned where all the best hiding places were in the small trailer: under the bed, behind the couch, in the low cabinet in the kitchen that she could easily hook open with her claw. The humans frequently forgot to feed her, so Anca stayed small. Over the growling of her belly, she reminded herself that at least she was not outgrowing the best hiding spots.

One day, after a particularly strident screaming match, the brittle woman left and did not come back, and Anca was left alone in the company of the sour-smelling man. She mourned the loss of the brittle woman only because the woman remembered to feed her more often than the man did.

He often left the door unlatched, and Anca was able to slip into the night and do some hunting for herself and thus keep from starving. At least the rodents were plentiful in the warm springtime air. In her nighttime prowls, Anca kept watch for the human she had been promised, but no human in the trailer park showed her any kindness. If they did not ignore her, they flung garbage and harsh words at her. Anca began to feel the cold tendrils of despair creep into her heart. She lifted her heart to the sky and cried out to The Great Mother.

"Where is she? Where is the human you promised me?" The anguish in her voice silenced the chorus of insects around her.

"Soon," said The Great Mother. "She is not ready yet, but you will meet her soon."

Anca slunk away, trying to clutch some hope in her heart, her belly low in misery.

In time, her heat came upon her, and one of the neighborhood toms was more than happy to put kittens in her belly. Anca looked forward to the joy of kittens, but when the sour-smelling man saw that her belly was swelling, he took a broom and beat her with it. He chased her from one end of the trailer to the other, unrelenting. Whatever hiding place she chose, he forced her from it with hard jabs from the handle. Relief only came when she scuttled from the trailer and away from his territory into the summer rain. And Anca was alone in the world, but for the kittens in her belly.

The wild was not forgiving to Anca in this lifetime. No feral colony would take her in, and she drove herself to exhaustion trying to care for her kittens and herself. Her body did not produce enough milk, and she watched two of her babies grow sickly and die as her own rickety frame grew smaller and smaller.

Again, she cried out to the sky, "Where is she? You promised!"

"Soon," said The Great Mother. "Very soon, my child."

Anca buried her face in her paws and allowed herself a moment to mourn her lost kittens, and then, she got on with the business of living. She tried to hold on to the hope of The Great Mother's promise, but it was a slippery thing, and she could not keep her paws around it.

When the first kind human Anca had ever met found her, she was delirious with hunger and fever, hiding under a holly bush with her remaining kittens. Even though Anca snarled and scratched, the human did not grow angry. She handled Anca with gentle hands and took her inside. Anca had no clear memory of the following weeks. She knew she was given some kind of medicine and that the kind human dribbled gruel down her throat, but the rest passed in a fever dream.

When her fever finally broke, she found that only one of the five kittens she birthed was still alive, and she sank down under the weight of her grief. She found a broad windowsill in the house of the kind human and made her place there. It became her world; there was no reason to leave. The kind human sometimes petted her and spoke in soothing tones. There was plentiful food, somehow, in this house full of cats. It was not what she had been promised, but it was better than she had ever had. It would have to do.

"This is only a weigh station," said an older tuxedo male. "Don't get too comfortable."

Anca ignored him and watched a black bird with a fountain pen clutched in his claws fly past her window. She watched the seasons cycle and change. One night she asked the moon, "Where is she?" in a cracked and whispery voice.

"Soon," was the answer. "She is almost here."

Anca tried to believe. She wanted to. But hope slipped out of her paws. There were worse places to be, and Anca settled down into a life on the windowsill.

So it was that when she finally did arrive, Anca was not looking for her. Anca heard the door open and close, and human voices chattering away, but it meant nothing to her. The kind human sometimes had guests, but it never disturbed Anca's rhythm.

"Here she is," said the kind human as she neared Anca's windowsill. Anca looked up with slitted eyes, expecting nothing. But there she was. To other humans, she was probably plain. Medium brown hair of average length; the same brown eyes that most humans had; average height: there was nothing special on the surface of this human. But when Anca Saw her, she glowed.

At first, Anca could not believe her eyes. After so long, after so much, there she stood, quietly glowing. She reached out her hand to let Anca sniff her.

"Hello, pretty girl, may I pet you?" Her voice was neither high nor low.

Anca head butted her and looked for a way to climb into her arms. Her human picked her up, and Anca nestled down into her arms and began to purr as she had only purred for The Great Mother before. Both of the humans laughed.

"It's like she was waiting for you," said the kind one.

"Yes," said Anca's human. "Yes, I think she was."

And so, Anca went home with her human. It was a small place, but it was neat and tidy, and there was already another cat there, a well-fed, older orange tabby. He sniffed her over and said, "So, you're finally here. Mother's been telling me to expect you for quite some time."

"I thought I would be here sooner," said Anca as she washed her face with her paw. "But our human did not come."

"Ah yes," he said. "She needed some time to heal. You were not the only one with wounds. I was to heal her so that she could come to you."

"Ah," said Anca, and she straightened her whiskers.

"Would you like to see where the best sunbeams are?"

"Yes, I would," said Anca. "I would like that very much."

# The Washer at the Laundromat

Bill's uniform shirts still looked dirty under the fluorescent lights, even though she knew very well that she'd just finished washing them. Polyester never looked clean and crisp like cotton. She folded them neatly into the basket, the last of his office uniforms from the bottom of the hamper, trying to minimize the wrinkles to iron out at home. They would hang clean in the closet until he returned, a year at least, possibly more, if she was lucky. A little shudder took her shoulders when she thought of what coming home early meant.

"You okay, Karen?" a tired looking brunette from across the folding table said.

"I'm fine, Bonnie," Karen said as she tucked a random auburn lock behind her ear. "Just letting my mind wander where it shouldn't. Why are laundromats so damned depressing?"

"I think it's some kind of law of physics," Bonnie laughed with little humor.

"So, have you and Charlie had any luck moving off base?" Karen asked.

Bonnie shrugged. "We'll need to sock away a little more of Charlie's combat pay before we can even consider a down payment. You?"

"I know this won't be Bill's last station. It seems silly to buy when I know we'll be somewhere else in a couple of years." Karen sighed.

Bonnie nodded. "Hey, do you want to go for a drink with some of the other wives after we're done? I've been asking everyone. We'll have a hen party."

"Sounds great," Karen glanced to the corner of the laundromat. "Did you ask her?"

"Don't look at her." Bonnie hissed. Her hands trembled as she folded a pair of her son's jeans.

"What? Why?" Karen twitched a little as she fought between getting a better look at the shadowy woman in the corner and following Bonnie's instructions.

"No one looks at her, no one talks to her." Bonnie's voice was tight and low.

"That's awful! What did she do?" Karen leaned into the table, the t-shirt in her hands forgotten.

"After she comes in here, men come home in boxes. Did you notice what she's washing?"

Karen shook her head.

"Uniforms," Bonnie said. "She's washing uniforms. And the men they belong to don't come home alive."

Karen looked back over her shoulder to see the woman shifting an armload of olive drab from a washer to a dryer. The woman began to raise her head and Karen whipped back around before they could make eye contact.

"That's crazy. How can a woman doing laundry mean anything to our guys half a world away?" Karen finally folded the t-shirt.

"I don't know. No one knows." Bonnie paired up some of her daughter's socks. "All we know is that after she comes in here and washes uniforms, we wind up with more widows." Bonnie wadded up the last of her unfolded laundry and stuffed it on top of her basket. "Let's get out of here. Being around her gives me the creeps."

"Okay," Karen said as she tossed the last few unfolded shirts on top of her basket and shifted it from the table to her hip.

Karen and Bonnie hustled out of the laundromat without another word. Bonnie stared resolutely forward, but at the door Karen looked back over her shoulder. This time, she and the mystery woman did make eye contact. The woman's black eyes had no white. They were cold and hard like a bird of prey. Karen shivered and let the door slap shut on the brightly lit laundromat, empty save for one woman and her basket of uniforms.

The word came the next day. A Fort Meade based unit escorting medical supplies was taken out by a roadside bomb. Five dead, three severely wounded. Four of the five dead had wives on base. Just as Bonnie had said, each basket of uniforms the bird-eyed woman washed brought a new crop of widows.

Weeks later, Karen wandered back into the empty laundromat in a fog. She paid no attention to the world around her as she loaded up two washers, one with colors and one with whites. She sat back in one of the red plastic chairs that lined the plate glass window in the front, the gossip magazine she meant to read held loosely in her lap. She was pregnant. The very personal farewell celebration she and Bill had had just before he left had taken root.

Part of her was thrilled. She'd always wanted children. She knew Bill would be a wonderful dad. But part of her was scared witless. Bill was half a world away and not expected back until well after the baby was due. Sure, her mother and her sister would help as much as they could, but there was only so much they could do from North Carolina to Maryland. They'd probably arrange their vacation time from work so that one of them could be with her for the birth and the other could be there to help her for a week or so after. Karen's thoughts skittered around between practical matters, like potential birthing coaches and baby clothes, and more fanciful things, like nursery decorations and stunning pre-school scores.

Her reverie was broken by the slap of the laundromat door. Karen looked up, hoping that Bonnie or one of her other friends was here so she could share her wonderful news. No such luck. It was the washer woman, with basket of dirty uniforms on her hip. Karen swallowed hard and fumbled with her magazine, pretending that she didn't feel the cool gaze of the woman on her. Karen held herself stiff and stared at the magazine pages with unseeing eyes, her knuckles white and trembling. Karen heard her footsteps, heard the basket set lightly on the floor, heard the washer dial turn and the cycle begin. She finally turned the page of the magazine she was pretending to read. Her hand trembled so badly she tore the page.

Karen tried to keep her breathing normal, tried to not listen to her legs that screamed at her to just leave the machines full of her sopping wet clothes and run. It was more than just the rumors she had heard about this woman, it was more than the experience of a few weeks ago.

Waves of fear seemed to roll off the washer woman like a tide. She managed to turn a page without ripping it, but she still hadn't read a word. She could hear the other woman breathing somewhere close by, slow and even and slightly hoarse.

Karen dared a glance up. The woman was perched on the machine she had filled, the one right next to the one loaded with Karen's whites. She was watching Karen with expressionless black eyes. Cold and fear flowing from the woman's eyes rolled through Karen. Karen gasped and ducked back down into her magazine. She sat, staring at the magazine in her lap, listening to the washing machines whir, not daring to look up again.

Karen jumped when the alarm sounded on her machine full of colors. She still didn't move. Two minutes later the alarm on her machine full of whites buzz. She stuffed a whimper down her throat and glanced up from underneath her eyelashes. The woman was still perched on her machine and still watching, one eyebrow quirked in question. Karen took a deep breath and tossed her magazine on the chair next to her and got up to switch her laundry.

She moved as quickly as she could, her head down, scuttling between the washers and dryers. She stuffed the last bit of her whites into a dryer and fed it quarters when she heard the woman's washer buzz. Karen found herself drifting closer, as if her body wasn't her own, as the woman unloaded the wet uniforms, the sodden fabric slapping into the basket. It was a large load.

Karen was close, she could almost feel the body heat from the woman's skin. She glanced down at the basket. She could see the name tags on three of the uniform shirts - Meyers, Chandler, and Briggs. A strangled cry lodged in her throat and she snatched the shirt that bore her husband's name and before she could even think she was running for the door. Behind her she heard an angry caw.

The washer woman's hands dug into Karen's shoulders like claws and spun her around.

"Give me back what is mine," said the woman in a low, gravelly voice.

"You can't have him," whispered Karen, her t-shirt growing wet where she clutched the soaking fabric to her body. "I won't let you have him."

The washer woman would not let go of her shoulders. "You know what I do?"

"I know when you wash the uniforms, men come home in boxes. I don't want my husband to come home in a box."

"An understandable sentiment." The washer woman nodded. "However, I must finish my task, and you must give me back the shirt."

"Why? Why do you have to do this to us?"

"It is the way of things," the woman blinked. "There are wars, soldiers die, I wash to send them on. Would you rather a world of deathless corpses?"

"No," Karen shuddered. "But I don't want my husband to die, or be hurt. We're having a baby." Her voice dropped to a whisper.

"Then choose another," said the woman as she spun Karen to face the rest of the laundromat.

There were about half a dozen women Karen didn't know. Their faces were slightly familiar from seeing them around the base, but she didn't know their names, or if they had children, or if they were happy in their marriages.

"Take a shirt from another's basket," the woman whispered in her ear. "And I will let you keep this one. No harm will come, this time."

The washer woman's released her clutch and Karen took two unsteady steps toward the other women. She glanced back at the washer woman and her stomach clenched tight. She bolted for the door with no idea where she was going, her eyes blinded with tears. She broke hard to the right and ran into the night with the wet shirt clutched close to her chest. Her feet slapped the pavement and sobs hitched up in her throat, her heart beat one word in her temples and chest: no, no, no, no. She heard cawing and wing beats behind her and glanced back just in time to dodge the biggest crow she'd ever seen in her life going straight for her head. She cried out and stumbled, skinning her bare knees on the sidewalk. She scrambled to her feet as the bird came about and headed right back for her. Karen darted off the sidewalk and into the open field that bordered the strip mall. Her breath was coming ragged gasps, sawing painfully in and out of her chest. Her thighs ached and her knees burned.

The bird hit her in the left shoulder and sent her sprawling into the grass and weeds. Karen rolled over onto her back and saw the crow coming right back for her. She raised the shirt up to protect her head and face. The crow's talons grasped the shirt, not Karen, and tried to yank the shirt from her grasp. Karen pulled the shirt close to her chest and rolled to her side to keep it away from the bird.

"No, no, no, no," she gasped, her voice barely coming in a whisper.

The bird released the fabric rather than be thrown to the ground and landed a short distance away. Karen watched with astonished eyes as the bird melted up into the shape of a woman, the woman washing uniforms at the Laundromat.

"Give me the shirt," she croaked with a gravelly voice.

"No," Karen sobbed. "You can't have it. I won't let you make me a widow." Hot tears began to roll down her face.

"You wish to save your man?" She cocked her head to the side.

"Yes, please," Karen whimpered.

"A trade then, your man for the babe in your belly."

"What?" Karen choked.

"I will guarantee that your man will not die in war if you give me the life of the child in your belly." The woman held out her hand.

"Who are you? What are you?"

"I am the Morrigan. I am one of the Sidhe, the rulers of the Fairie realm." The woman's voice was calm and even. "I hold dominion over the battlefield, and I can ensure that your man comes to no harm there."

Karen stared at her in wide-eyed shock. Her mind raced through the possibilities. The man she loved or the child she had never met? An innocent child or a grown man who had already had a chance at life? Karen buried her face into the stiffening shirt and sobbed.

"I can't," she gasped. "I can't."

"Then give me what is mine. You have no rights here." The Morrigan held out her hand again.

Karen clutched the shirt to her for just a moment more, then reluctantly offered it with trembling hands. The Morrigan took it and laid it over her arm. Karen turned her face to the side and shut her eyes.

"Your man will die before your child. Isn't that as it should be?"

Karen heard the downbeat of wings and rolled over into the grass, sobbing.

The word came late the next day. It was bad. A suicide bomber using a child as a decoy attacked a roadside checkpoint. Eight dead, five wounded, and two of the wounded were not expected to live. None of them were Karen's husband.

It wasn't long before Karen saw the Morrigan in the laundromat again. It was late on a Tuesday and she and Bonnie were companionably folding laundry and chatting. The Morrigan moved through silently, a chill following after her. Karen watched her load a washer in the far corner of the laundromat. She noted with relief that it was a smaller load this time.

"Don't look at her," Bonnie whispered. "It's safer not to look at her."

"Actually, I talked to her," Karen said absently as she folded a pillow case and watched the Morrigan. "And it didn't kill me or Bill."

"I can't believe you did that," Bonnie gasped.

Karen nodded, and flipped the folded pillow case into her basket. "I'll be right back," she said and started to walk to where the Morrigan sat, perched on her washer and watching nothing with a blank stare.

"Karen, don't!" Bonnie said in a strangled whisper, reaching out with a useless hand.

Karen stood in front of the Morrigan and crossed her arms across her chest. The Morrigan slowly focused her eyes and looked at Karen. She cocked her head to one side.

"Was not our business concluded?" her voice came out in a croak.

"My husband's shirt was in your last load, but he wasn't on the list of the dead. How long are you going to torture me?"

"Was it really your husband's shirt?" The Morrigan cocked her head to the other side.

"It has his name on it." Karen's chin lifted a notch.

"Did it really? His whole name?" The Morrigan's mouth quirked up on the side.

"Well, no, just his last name. Meyers."

"Is he the only man in your army with that name?"

The blood drained from Karen's face. "No."

"And even so," the Morrigan said. "A Meyers was taken, just not your Meyers."

"But you said to me that my man would die before my child." Karen's hands fluttered over her still flat belly.

"Isn't that the natural way of things? The parent dies before the child?" She smiled a chilly smile.

"So Bill won't die over there?"

"I didn't say that." The Morrigan shrugged. "There is only so far that I can see. Your man is not in this basket, that is all I can tell you."

"But you told me you could control the battlefield," Karen said. "You need to keep your promise."

"I may be able to control things, but I do not see what is to come. That is not my bailiwick. But as much as is in my control, your man will be safe."

Karen's shoulders dropped with relief and she released a breath she didn't realize she was holding. The washer buzzed and the Morrigan hopped off to switch the uniforms to the dryer. She pulled out one shirt and stroked the tag with her thumb. Karen could not see what it said.

"Soon, perhaps, you should be ready to comfort your friend over there." The Morrigan's eyes were as black and unreadable as ever. And without another word she turned to finish her task.

# The Escape of Baba Yaga

When she drew in a breath, it stung the inside of her nose. It wasn't supposed to do that. And her own bed was not hard and angled as this one was, with stiff sheets stretched tight over her legs. She tried to throw them off and found she was bound to the bed, and there was a strange tube coming from her arm. What manner of witchery was this? She cast back in her cloudy mind, trying to piece together what she was doing in this unfamiliar place, but all she could remember was tucking into her own bed safe and sound, the comforter she made with her own hands drawn up to her chin, and sliding into sweet dreams. And then there was a great gaping blackness in her memory. And then here. Baba Yaga felt frightened and helpless. She didn't like the alien feelings one little bit.

She strained against her bonds, sawing back and forth, letting her mind wander with the rhythm of her body, trying to figure a way out. As she rocked and strained, she heard voices outside of the darkened room.

"It's no big deal," said a hoarse feminine whisper. "She's been here for years; being late on one shot isn't going to kill her. Not that I think it would matter to that nephew of hers." There was a snort.

"You get paid to follow instructions," grumbled a low male voice. "It may not matter with this one, but what about the others? What if you miss a critical dose with one of them? Some of them have families that care, you know."

"Get off my case. I'm giving it to her now, okay?"

Yaga heard a door creak.

"What were you doing anyway?" The voices were coming closer to the bed, and Yaga twisted her head to the side trying to see, but she was barred by railing up the side. This was most certainly not her bed.

"None of your business," mumbled the female voice.

Yaga could finally make them out in the dim light of the room. The girl was slight, with mousy brown hair pulled back into a ponytail.

She wore loose, bright pink trousers and a loose blouse that seemed to be decorated with children's scrawlings. The man had dark hair, cut severely short, with glasses and a great white coat with a name stitched on his chest. The girl carried a hypodermic in her hand, and she reached for Yaga's arm.

"Ungh!" Yaga tried to scream stop but all that came from her throat was a rusty croak. But that was enough. The girl snatched back her hand and yelped. The man stared in slack-jawed disbelief.

"What was that about a late shot not making a difference?" he said.

Yaga thrashed against her bonds like a trout and tried to force her voice out again. "Let me go." The thin whisper trickled from her.

"Now, dear, please don't strain like that. You'll hurt yourself." The man said as he set his hands against Yaga's shoulders and tried to press her back into the bed.

She struggled harder. "Curse you." Her voice was stronger this time.

"Mrs. Yaga! If you don't settle down, we'll sedate you." He was pressing her down harder and almost shouting. "Mary, go get the sedative," he said without turning to the girl, who fled the room wide-eyed.

"Let me go! You have no right! I'll curse your house."

She heard the door slap open, and the girl breathlessly said, "Here."

"You'll feel better in a minute." The man took his hands from her shoulders, and there was fumbling with the tube coming out of her arm.

A heavy lassitude stole over Yaga, and her struggles grew more and more feeble. The man must have a powerful sleeping potion, thought Yaga as consciousness slipped away.

When she woke again, the sun was shining, and Yaga could see the room around her. It was a sterile, austere affair with pale pea green walls. Yaga tried to move but found she was still tied to the bed. Now, it held her in a near sitting position. Someone had moved her.

Yaga's eyes traced over modern conveniences. Prodding her murky mind, she found names for them all: a telephone on the night table just out of reach; a television, on and mumbling softly, bolted to the wall; an air conditioner that made the sheer beige curtains flutter. She remembered when each new miracle was invented, popularized, and eventually taken for granted. Even in the far reaches of the taiga forest, where she preferred to spend most of her time these days, everyone had heard of, seen, or used things like telephones, televisions, and air conditioners. She heard the door creak, and a tall, lanky blond man entered with a tray.

"Good morning, Mrs. Yaga," he said in a thick, nasally voice. "Time for breakfast. We have broth!" Smiling, he set the tray on the tall table at her side.

She looked at his blue eyes, set a little too close together, and thought, a simpleton. I can use this to my advantage. Yaga stretched her mouth into the seldom used shape of a welcoming smile.

"What is your name, dear?" She tried to make her dusty croak sound as sweet as a bird in springtime.

"My name is Johnny." His grin grew even wider as he took the cover off a bowl of steaming broth. He took a spoonful and blew gently on it. "Ready, Mrs. Yaga?"

"Call me Babushka, dear. It means grandmother," she said, then sipped down the salty liquid he offered her. She was proud that she managed not to choke. Her own soup was much better than this swill.

"Okay, Babushka." He held another spoonful.

"Can you take these off?" She held up her hands as far as they would go.

"Oh no." Johnny's eyes grew very wide, and his hand trembled and slopped broth on the covers. "Mary would be so mad at me. I'm not supposed to do anything but what she says." As if just remembering his task, he thrust the spoon into old woman's face.

Yaga swallowed the broth. "Oh, please. I promise I'll be good. I won't get you in any trouble." She swallowed another spoonful to prove her point.

Johnny frowned and shook his head, then held out another spoonful. Yaga slurped that up, too.

"If you let me go, I could feed myself," she said. "You could go enjoy some sun."

Johnny looked toward the room's single narrow window and licked his lips.

"Mary would never have to know. Whether you feed me or I feed myself, the broth will still be gone," Yaga wheedled.

"Well, if Mary never finds out..."

"Yes! Mary will never find out." She held very still.

He bit his lip and turned to the window again. "You better not get me in trouble," he said as he released Yaga's straps.

"No, no trouble at all. Now, go play, my boy." She sat up straighter and chafed her wrists.

Johnny bobbed his head and left the room with a smile on his face. As soon as the door clicked shut, Yaga yanked the tube from her arm and winced at the momentary pinch. She pressed her finger onto the tiny wound and surveyed her surroundings again with a less muddled mind. The longer she was away from whatever the man had put in her arm the night before, the clearer her thinking became. She had heard of places like this: "assisted living facilities" or "old folk's homes." Prisons are more like it, Yaga thought as she swung her bare feet onto the cold tile floor. No matter, she would not be here long. Her head swam a bit, then cleared.

Yaga shook her stooped and wizened body, loosening up and preparing for magic. She raised her arms, tilted her head back, and closed her eyes. She would call her chicken legged hut and be gone before Mary realized what Johnny had done and beat him for it. Yaga reached out for her power and found nothing. There was a wall instead of a door, and she hadn't the strength to push it. Lifting her hands and straining harder, beads of sweat popped out on her upper lip. Still nothing. The woman dropped to her knees, gasping. Something was wrong with her magic, that much was obvious. Normally, calling the hut required about as much power as twitching her little finger. Yaga dropped her chin to her chest and growled. Whoever had done this to her, whoever had imprisoned her, had done a fine job. But there were other ways around things; she would not admit defeat yet.

She climbed back up onto the bed and slurped down the rest of the now stone-cold broth. When she was done, she used what stickiness was left on the medical tape to lightly tack the IV back down without putting it her arm. She fastened her own ankle restraints and laid back and wrapped the wrist restraints loosely enough to easily slip out. No need for any of the powers that be to know she could leave her padded cage. After moonrise, she'd find a way out. No walls could hold Baba Yaga.

Moonrise came, and Yaga crept out of her room to find her prison quiet. The night nurse slept at her station, a half-finished romance novel loosely held against her chest. The other inmates slept or moaned fitfully in their rooms. Yaga's bare feet made no sound on the gleaming white linoleum. She found the office with no trouble and hoped that something in the paperwork kept there would give her a clue as to why her magic would not work. Yaga smiled when she tested the office door, unlocked. Apparently, her jailors never expected their charges to be up and about at night.

The faux wood file cabinets in the far corner of the room held what she was looking for. By the bright moonlight streaming in through the curtainless window, she flicked through the thick, dull green folders until she found one labeled Yaga, Baba. She snorted. Whatever fool locked her in here hadn't even bothered to give her a false name. Baba wasn't even a proper name, merely a title, and not a very polite one at that. Then again, most of the world didn't even tell the old stories any more. Why should they believe that the characters from those stories actually existed?

Yaga lowered herself stiffly to the floor and leafed through her file. She was supposed to be in a persistent vegetative state, and a special sedative was to be administered every 12 hours to help her live out her final days in comfort and peace. And her final days had been going on for the last five years. The calming drug was prescribed by a doctor outside the facility and was delivered by courier once a week. Yaga wondered what the local quacks were going to do now that she was awake. Who would they call? She continued to flip through the file.

And then she found it, the name of the person who had imprisoned her. Her admission paperwork listed her nephew as her legal guardian, one Koschei Nickolayevich Bessmertniy. Yaga's breath whistled past her teeth. How could the old bastard get away with claiming Nickolai as a father? Or any father for that matter? And the memories flooded back.

Koschei, as was usual for him, had pursued a sweet young girl and tried to make her his. Yaga couldn't blame the child for running. She had every right not to want Koschei's skeletal, deathless hands on her. So she came to Baba Yaga to beg for protection; Vasilisa Prekrasnaya was her name. Little Vasilisa eagerly agreed to Baba Yaga's price, and so Yaga wove her a spell of protection that even Koschei could not break. And it had worked beautifully. Koschei was livid at first, but after a few decades, his anger seemed to cool, and he brought Yaga a conciliatory bottle of vodka to congratulate her on outwitting him. They toasted each other by the fire in Yaga's chicken-legged hut, and then, she woke up here. She pursed her lips. Now was the time to call in her payment from Vasilisa's bargain. But first, she would need a few things.

Back in her room, Baba took a saucer and laid it on the floor in a patch of moonlight. She placed a slice of white bread in it, and as she poured a carton of milk over it, she chanted.

"Vasilisa's Domovoi, please come into this house and tend the flocks!

"Vasilisa's Domovoi, please come into this house and serve me well!

"Vasilisa's Domovoi, please come into this house and pay your debt!"

The creature that came snuffling out of the baseboard a few moments later was covered in wiry gray hair and had little nibs of horns on his forehead and a short tail that switched back and forth like a cat's. If he stood tall, he would have reached a small child's waist, but he walked slightly stooped, like he would drop down to all fours at any moment. He swept a deep bow to Baba Yaga. His pink tongue darted out and licked his black lips above his pointed little chin. "May I eat, Babushka?"

"You may," Yaga allowed as she sat back on her heels.

The little domovoi smacked his lips, then ripped great hunks of sopping bread and stuffed them in his cheeks. When he was done, he patted his belly and belched.

"I was beginning to think you would never call in your end of the bargain. But the domovoi of Vasilisa's house always uphold the bargains made by their mistress, even though the travel wearies me. A domovoi should never be far from home. No matter. How may I serve you, Baba Yaga?"

"I need help and information. This may be a long task," Yaga warned.

"Long or short, it is all the same. The bargain was struck and must be honored." The domovoi bowed again.

Yaga sighed. "I need to escape this place, and my magic is not working."

He whistled. "That is very bad indeed. Let's have a look at you." The domovoi crawled into Yaga's lap and stood on her knees to begin his examination. He looked deep into both eyes, up her nose, and down her throat, then held the sides of her head as he peered into each ear in turn. He hopped off her lap and paced the room as he stroked his chin. His tail snapped back and forth in agitation.

"It seems whatever poison is in your blood has blunted your magic. I believe it will come back, but it will take time," he said.

"I don't have time," hissed Yaga. "I have to get out of here before they give me more medicine, and I must find Koschei and punish him for what he has done to me."

"I don't know what to tell you, Babushka." The domovoi shrugged. "I can't make your magic come back."

Yaga and the domovoi faced each other in the moonlight, one set of eyes angry, one set of eyes sad. Then Yaga happened upon a solution.

"Aha!" she crowed. "Does not your mistress have a magical doll that grants wishes?"

"She does," the domovoi allowed, trying to look anywhere but at Yaga's eyes. "But I can't be sure where it is right this very moment."

"Don't lie to me," Yaga whispered. The domovoi's shoulders slumped, and he was still.

"My mistress will be very angry with me for taking her doll." Yaga could barely hear his voice.

"I only need to borrow it, not keep it," Yaga said.

"If you only borrow it, there is a limit to the wishes, Babushka."

"How many do I get?"

"Three."

"That will be enough. Bring me the doll," Yaga ordered.

"As you wish, Babushka." The domovoi bowed. "I will bring it between moonset and dawn tomorrow."

Yaga nodded. "Swift travels to you, good friend."

"Sweet dreams, Babushka." And the domovoi disappeared.

The next night in the dark after moonrise, Baba Yaga crept from her room again to roam her prison's halls. She had too much nervous energy to stay put, and the house spirit wouldn't arrive until after moonset, after all. There was a different nurse asleep at the desk tonight, but it seemed she was reading the same novel, and it had fallen from her slack fingers onto the floor. Yaga padded up and down the halls, driven to move but having nothing useful to move toward.

As she passed one room, she heard a moan. Out of morbid curiosity, she slid in to the room on little cat feet. There was only one occupied bed. It was a wizened old skeleton, barely covered in skin with one wild tuft of fluffy white hair flying off the top of her head. It had perhaps once been a beautiful woman: the cheekbones were certainly lovely. But surely it could not be alive, Yaga thought. And then it - she - moaned again. Yaga saw her eyes were open, eyes that might once have been the blue of sweet summer skies but were now the sullen gray of the end of the year. Those eyes, so full of pain, locked on Yaga. One withered claw rose up off the bed.

"Help me," came the weakened breath from shriveled lips.

Yaga leaned closer. "How?"

"Kill me."

Yaga looked over all the wires and tubes that flowed from the creature to the beeping and buzzing machines that were keeping her alive. If she had her magic, it would be a small thing to send out a jolt that would make the machines stop working. Magic and technology were not friendly neighbors. Yaga reached into herself to see if there was enough magic to accomplish this small mercy. She could feel a few feeble tendrils deep inside her, but there was not enough.

"I'm sorry," Yaga said as she backed away for the door. The dying woman's eyes followed her. The sound that escaped the woman's lips would have been a wail of anguish if there had been enough strength in her body for it.

When the moon finally set and the domovoi slunk out from the baseboard again, Baba Yaga nearly pounced on him with delight. The doll he had wrapped in his arms was nearly as big as he was. It was an old-fashioned thing, worn but well cared for, dressed in the traditional costume of a woman from the Russian steppes. Yaga snatched it from the domovoi's hands.

"No bread and milk this time?" The domovoi pouted.

"You'll have all the bread and milk you want as soon as I have my magic back." Yaga stroked the doll's blonde hair with greedy fingers. "One little wish, and all will be right with the world."

"No!" cried the domovoi as he tried to leap up and grab the doll from Yaga. She held it up just a little out of reach.

"What do you mean, no? You said I could have three wishes if I only borrowed it. I only want one; I just want to wish my magic back."

"You can't do that." The little domovoi huffed and puffed. "It is too powerful a wish! You would destroy the doll completely. Oh dear, Mistress will be so vexed with me." He wrung his hands and tears gathered in the corners of his eyes.

Yaga lowered her hands slightly but kept a firm grip on the doll. "Well, I certainly wouldn't want to destroy something so precious, but I may have to. I have to escape this prison." She paused. "Unless there is something you can offer me in exchange."

"Anything, Babushka. Please don't make me return to my mistress and tell her I allowed her most precious possession to be destroyed." The domovoi whimpered, and his lip trembled.

"If you were to offer me service," Yaga crooned as she stroked the doll, "I may be convinced to restrain my desires."

"A year," the domovoi said. "A year of smiling service, of doing anything you wish."

"A year for each wish, three years total." Yaga's eyes thinned to slits, and the corner of her mouth quirked up.

"Three years!" wailed the little domovoi. "Oh, my sweet mistress will be so angry."

"What would make her more angry, my pet? Losing your service for a time, or losing the doll forever?"

"You drive a hard bargain, Baba Yaga. But I accept it." The domovoi spit in his palm and held his hand out. Yaga did the same, and they slapped their palms together.

"Agreed!" cackled Yaga. "No, how far can I go without damaging the doll?"

"Make a specific wish that only requires a small amount of magic," the domovoi said. Yaga rubbed her whiskery chin, deep in thought.

"Aha!" She held the doll up in the air with both hands. "I wish my chicken-legged hut would come to me so that I can leave this place." She enunciated each word. There must be no confusion. Yaga waited, barely daring to breathe. The night ticked by in silence.

"I do not hear the footsteps of my hut, Domovoi. Have you played me false?" Her voice was tight and sharp.

"No, Babushka, no! The doll is real, and your wish will come true. Reach out with your heart with the love you have for your hut. What do you feel?"

Yaga thought of her cozy bed, her hearth that was ever warm, her rocking chair that led many a restless soul to sound and restorative sleep. And she felt it, the tug to the East.

"It's coming! It's coming!" she crowed, then sighed. "It has many miles to walk and an ocean to swim. But it should be here by morning."

"See Babushka! All will be well." The domovoi smiled like the sun. "While we wait, perhaps we should have some milk and bread."

"Patience, I have another wish to make." Yaga raised the doll again. "I wish for a trinket that will always and without fail point me to wherever that bastard Koschei is."

She lowered the doll, and there was a cold shiver in the air. Around the doll's neck was a sleek silver chain, and on that chain was a silver compass, with the needle pointing North West. Yaga paced around the room and shifted the doll and its trinket this way and that, but the needle always pointed in the same direction. Yaga chuckled to herself and slipped the chain from the doll's neck and placed it on her own.

"What will you wish for next?" The domovoi rocked back and forth on his toes.

"I don't know yet," Yaga said in a voice soft and wistful.

"Perhaps we shall have milk and bread then?"

"We shall have milk and bread." Yaga patted the domovoi on his head, and they crept from her room and let their noses lead them to the kitchen.

As they slipped back through the empty halls, the domovoi with his belly swollen from all the milk and bread he could hold, Yaga paused in front of the room where the shell of a woman rested. She stood in the hall and listened to the soft sounds of pain coming from the cracked door. The old woman petted the doll clutched in her fist. The domovoi tugged on the edge of her nightgown.

"What is it, Babushka? Are you all right?"

"We are close to dawn, yes?"

"The sun will crest the horizon in a few minutes," he said.

Yaga reached out with her hidden sense and found her hut striding across the landscape. It was close. It would arrive moments after dawn. Yaga nodded to herself. She could afford this small mercy, and she pushed open the door to the room of pain.

The woman's eyes tracked her and widened more when she caught sight of the domovoi clinging to Baba Yaga's hem.

"Babushka, what are we doing in here? It smells of death, and I don't like it," the domovoi whined.

"Hush, Domovoi. We only have one small errand here." She looked down on the creature in the bed but could not bring herself to touch her; instead, she just spoke. "I have come to do as you ask. I have come to free you."

The only answer Yaga got was an exhalation of breath and softening at the corners of the woman's eyes. She raised the doll for a third and final time and spoke with a clear voice. "I wish this woman to be free of her tethers and for her spirit to fly to its final rest."

Yaga and the domovoi counted three slow heartbeats, then, one by one, each machine popped, and in showers of sparks and streams of smoke, they stopped working. The woman breathed her last, her eyes fluttered shut, and her lips curved up ever so slightly. Yaga smiled herself while the alarms began to shriek and wail.

"Babushka, we must go," the domovoi cried as he pulled her toward the door.

Yaga and the domovoi stumbled out into the hall, coughing and gasping. The doctor came skidding around the corner, his hair wild and white coat all askew, with Nurse Mary close behind.

"You," he roared as he pointed to Baba Yaga. "How did you get out?"

"Run," cried Yaga to the domovoi. "The hut should be outside by now."

They fled down the hall, but her old legs and the domovoi's short legs were no match for the young, long legs of the doctor and Nurse Mary. The doctor and Nurse Mary were hard on their heels, fingers nearly grasping fabric, when Yaga and the domovoi burst out the back door. The crisp, cool air, almost cold enough to make their breath steam, slapped their cheeks. Johnny goggled at them from the bed of mums he was weeding as they ran by. He began to rise, a question on his lips, and the doctor pushed him back to the ground on his way past. But then he and Nurse Mary froze in shock.

There, on the back lawn of the hospital, was a cabin with no doors and no windows to be seen, standing on great, golden-feathered chicken legs. Baba Yaga was dancing and laughing at its feathered feet. She lifted up her arms and cried, "Turn your back to the forest, your front to me!"

The hut turned an impossible 180 degrees without moving its feet and bowed forward, revealing a door, which Baba Yaga and the domovoi leapt into with joy. Yaga hung out the door and cackled at her would-be captors. She reached behind her into the cabin and brought forth her hand.

"I told you I would curse your house if you did not release me. For you, you will live without love, and your family tree will wither with your branch." She cast a hard and wizened potato, with no life in it at all, and it struck the doctor in the forehead.

"For you, I curse you with the age you fear." She threw a bone china saucer at Nurse Mary, and it shattered on the crown of her head, gray strands spreading through her hair from it like ripples in a pond and wrinkles drawing down her screaming mouth.

"For your kindness, I give you the gift of thought." She tossed a spoon to Johnny, and it landed lightly in his hand. "Use it wisely."

Then Baba Yaga's hut turned neatly on nimble chicken feet and headed North West.

# The Fisherman's Bargain

Annie glanced at the scrap of notebook paper in her hand to make sure she had the right address. It was the right place, but the unassuming door of a basement apartment in the Seton Hill neighborhood of Baltimore didn't seem like the place to find magical help of any sort. But she took a deep breath and straightened her shoulders and knocked anyway. A young Asian woman with her glossy black hair bobbed short with lime green streaks answered the door.

"May I help you?" she said.

"Yes," said Annie. "I'm looking for Jenny."

"That's me." The woman smiled brightly. "What can I do for you?"

"Well, er... my friend, she... um... said that you might be able to help me?"

Jenny raised an eyebrow. "With what, hon?"

"It's kind of hard to talk about." Annie shuffled from foot to foot, swallowing hard and trying not to cry.

Before she knew what she was happening, Jenny drew her into the basement apartment by her hand and had her settled in the cozy kitchenette and sipping a hot cup of fragrant tea. The whole story came spilling out of her in a raging torrent: how she and her brother Charlie had been sailing on what seemed like a perfect day when a bad squall came up, and Charlie was sucked off the deck of their small boat by hungry waves. She had done everything she could to save him, but he had still drowned. Now, she had nightmares every night. Annie desperately wanted to sleep, but every time she tried, she saw his white face surrounded by thundering black water. The water always sucked him down, and the last thing Annie always saw was his beseeching hand. She could never reach him.

"I've tried everything: sleeping pills, antidepressants, therapy, and nothing works. So, my friend Lisbeth said you might be able to help me." Annie fixed her desperate eyes on Jenny.

Jenny reached for Annie's nearly empty cup and swirled the leaves, then turned it over with a sharp flick of her wrist. She drew the cup back slowly and examined the swirled mound of wet leaves on the Formica table. Shaking her head, she sighed.

"If Charlie had died any other way, we might have more options," Jenny began. "But since he drowned, there's really only one thing to do."

"What?" Annie leaned forward.

"It's dangerous, and it might not even work…"

"I don't care," said Annie. "I'll try anything."

"Just remember, you're the only one who can save him."

"Save him? From what?"

Jenny took deep breath and swayed a little, her voice coming out with an odd poetic cadence. "From the Fisherman, the King of the Dead Depths. Poor Charlie, all alone in that crab pot."

"Charlie can't be in a crab pot," Annie said. "He's dead. I saw him die."

"Of course he's dead." Jenny patted Annie's hand. "The Fisherman couldn't have trapped his soul otherwise."

"Charlie's trapped?" The blood drained out of Annie's face.

"Trapped by the Fisherman," Jenny closed her eyes and bit her lip. "His soul crammed into a crab pot in a cavern full of crab pots, a soul in every one. That's why you're having nightmares, hon. Charlie needs you to set him free."

Annie swallowed hard. "What do I have to do?"

"First you have to raise the Witch. She's the only one who can show you the way to the Fisherman. Only she knows how to get him to set a soul free."

"How do I raise the Witch?"

"Stay there."

Jenny pulled plastic tubs out of her kitchen cabinets and started in on her work. She selected a few bay leaves, a pinch of cat nip, and a small handful of hops, then crushed them one by one in an old stone mortar and pestle releasing a dry, pungent smell. Next, she mixed the crushed plants carefully with her fingertip, then tossed in a handful of salt. She measured out the resulting powder into six white paper envelopes the size of Annie's palm. The whole time, she whispered to herself in a language that Annie did not understand. When she was done, she handed Annie the small packets.

"Go into the woods and find an empty clearing," she instructed Annie. "Place one packet of the herbs into a bowl made of a pure substance and burn them. Before the smoke is done you must recite, 'Witch, I call thee. Witch, I beseech thee. Witch, I beg thee come to my aid' three times, and then, the Witch will come to you. Then you must present her with a gift that you have made yourself. Then, and only then, she might grant you what you seek. But I make no guarantees."

"What do I owe you?" Annie caressed the fine paper packets in her hand.

"You can't pay me for that. It's against The Way to charge for real magic. Good luck," she said and squeezed Annie's hand.

Annie crashed through the beech and yellow poplar in Druid Hill Park, brushing branches out of her face and cursing as she tugged her jeans loose from a stray deadfall. She finally stumbled out into a clearing, empty of everything save moonlight. Annie stood in the center of the clearing and turned around full circle. She was definitely alone. Far off in the distance, she could hear the hum of the traffic on Greenspring Avenue.

"Here goes nothing," she murmured and started to set out the packages she had brought. A pure white quartz bowl, purchased at the new age shop down the street from her apartment, glowed in the moonlight; the creamy white paper of the herb packet seemed to bask and absorb the light from the bowl when Annie placed it on the ground. She opened another package and placed a soft gray cardigan on the ground next the bowl. She had gotten it at J.C. Penney on a half off sale. While she hadn't made it herself, the tag did say hand knit, and she figured that would be good enough. Next, she poured the herbs into the bowl and pulled the matches from her pocket. Taking a deep breath, she struck the match and set the herbs on fire. As soon as she saw the first tendrils of smoke, she began to recite the chant Jenny had taught her.

As she finished it the third time, the air began to quiver and shiver in front of her. A white cottage with a thatched roof appeared. A gray tabby napping in an empty flowerbox opened one great yellow eye and observed Annie suspiciously. The red wooden door on the cottage flew open. An old woman in a brown homespun dress strode forth.

"Who dares disturb me?" she hissed.

"I do," Annie said, climbing to her feet. "I need your help."

"You brought a gift?"

"Yes." Annie held out the cardigan. The Witch snatched the sweater from Annie and sniffed it suspiciously.

"You didn't make this."

"Err, no. But it's hand knit."

"Go away," barked the Witch, and she retreated into the cottage. The cottage quivered again and disappeared before Annie could force her throat open.

The next night Annie returned to the clearing, this time with a plate of peanut butter cookies she baked herself. She burned the herbs and recited the chant, and once again, the air shivered and quivered, and the cottage appeared once more. This time, the tabby meowed at her. Once again, the door flew open, and the Witch strode out. She was wearing the gray cardigan Annie gave her the previous night.

"You again?" The Witch growled.

Annie held up the plate of cookies. "I made them myself, from scratch."

The Witch took the cookies and sniffed them. She took one and bit off a small corner.

"Not bad," she said. "What do you want?"

"I need your help to rescue my brother's soul from the Fisherman."

"Go away!" shrieked the Witch, tossing the plate back at Annie and scattering the cookies all over the ground. "I don't want to deal with that bastard ever again." The Witch retreated into her cottage, and for the second time, it disappeared without Annie being able to speak again.

Annie would not give up. She still had four packets of powder. And the nightmares still tortured her. The next night she arrived armed with a plate of double chocolate fudge with walnuts, her one and only culinary specialty. She was determined to get her way. Annie burned and chanted, and the air quivered and quavered, and the cottage appeared again, but the door remained stubbornly shut.

"Witch, I need your help!" Annie cried.

"Go away," came a muffled voice from inside the cottage.

"Whatever he did to you, I can help you get back at him."

The door creaked open a crack. The Witch's rheumy, gray eye peeked around the corner.

"You have my attention."

"Okay, well, he collects souls, right?" Annie began. "If I take one away from him, I'll at least make him mad, and maybe even embarrass him."

The door opened wider. "You're a persistent little snot, aren't you? Come in, and bring the fudge."

The cottage was packed to the brim with drying herbs; overstuffed furniture; and cats, lots and lots of cats. The gray tabby that Annie saw the two nights before rubbed her ankles and purred.

"Stop that, Midas," grumbled the Witch. "You're such a slut."

Annie started to sit down in one of the overstuffed chairs.

"I didn't invite you!" barked the Witch.

Annie shot up into a standing position, and the Witch snatched a piece of the fudge from her. Again, she sniffed and nibbled.

"Okay," she said. "I'm listening."

"I need your help to rescue my brother Charlie from the Fisherman, and I understand you're the only one who knows how to do it," Annie said.

"So what's in it for me?" The Witch gobbled down the hunk of fudge.

"You get to embarrass the heck out of him?"

"Not good enough." The Witch licked streaks of chocolate from her fingers.

"Doing a good deed for me will help your karma?"

"I'm immortal... what do I need with karma?" The Witch's hand hovered over the plate.

"I'm not leaving until you help me." Annie clutched the plate, white knuckled.

The Witch chewed slowly on another piece of fudge. "Fine, as long as you stop bugging me, and I can live in peace again." The Witch rummaged through the cubbyholes in an old roll-top desk and produced a small vial of thick green liquid.

"Drink this," said the Witch. "You have to drink it at midnight, then jump off the dock immediately or the air will suffocate you. Go straight to the Fisherman's lair where you must challenge him to a drinking game. If you out drink him, he will have to set your brother's soul free. The potion will give you some protection from the drink, but be careful. But watch him, he will try to sneak more into your cup."

Annie took the vial from her. "A drinking game underwater? How does that work?"

The Witch shrugged. "I enchanted a decanter and cups for him a few hundred years ago. They behave just like they do on land when you're underwater, but when you're on land they behave like they're underwater. He likes to use them for bar tricks when he comes ashore."

The Witch shooed Annie toward the door. Annie stopped in the doorway.

"But what if it doesn't work, or I mess it up?"

"If it doesn't work, wait for me on the docks, and I'll find you. We'll get your brother's soul from that old bastard one way or another."

The old woman pushed Annie out of the cottage.

"Do it soon," she called as she shut the door. "It will be easier if you do it soon."

The vial sat on the vanity in Annie's bedroom for three days. The nightmares continued but with one small change. Over the thundering waves, Annie could hear Charlie cry out, "Help me!" Annie started up from the nightmare for what seemed like the hundredth time.

"Screw this," she muttered as she pulled on sneakers and jeans. She grabbed the vial from the vanity on the way out the door. It was almost midnight, and she would have to hurry to get to the Inner Harbor on time.

Annie reached the head of the dock just as the clock in the Bromo Seltzer tower began to strike midnight. One, two, three...

Since there was no time to waste, she broke the wax seal on the vial as she jogged toward the water. Four, five, six...

She tossed back the potion and cast the vial away. Seven, eight, nine...

The air crushed down on her, and she couldn't breathe. Ten, eleven...

She stumbled the last two steps and dropped off the edge of the dock through the tendrils of autumn fog on the harbor. The last strike of the clock was swallowed by the frigid October water.

The water rushed past her, and she was dragged into a great torrent of current that drew her down, down, down far past what she knew the true depth of the harbor to be. Annie was shocked that she could breathe in the current, but then reconsidered the thought. The Witch had told her to get in the water immediately. Part of the potion must give her the ability to breathe underwater. The current finally dumped her at the mouth of a cave somewhere deep in unexplored water. Annie could not tell how far she had traveled.

This must be the place, she thought. She squared up her shoulders and did her best to stride boldly in. The mouth of the cave was just big enough to let her pass, but it quickly opened to a hall that put the grandest European cathedrals to shame. Every bit of wall space was covered with crab pots, thousands of them. The water around her brought a buzz to her ears. Annie rubbed both of her ears, thinking that the water pressure must be playing tricks on her. The buzzing resolved itself to voices, thousands of distinct voices all saying the same thing, "Help me."

"Who dares invade my lair?" boomed a voice from the shadowy recesses of the deepest part of the cave. "Who dares disturb my peace?" The Fisherman hobbled out of the shadows. He was stooped and had a hunch in his back. He shuffled forward leaning heavily on a driftwood staff, dressed in sail cloth rags. His long hair and beard was full of tangled kelp and swayed in the current of the cave. One eye was missing, and the other burned with green fire.

"I am Annie." Her voice trembled. "And I challenge you to a drinking game."

"What for?" he growled.

"A soul, the Witch told me I could get a soul."

"Damned old bat," he muttered. "Fine, fine. Let's get on with it."

He gestured to a large barrel and two smaller ones that served for table and chairs. Annie sat and the Fisherman produced a bottle of whiskey and two cups from under his sail cloth. He poured out equal measures and lifted his cup.

"To your health, girl. Here's hoping you lose." He drank it all in one gulp. Annie tossed back her own. The Witch was true to her word. The potion did offer some protection from the drink, and Annie matched the Fisherman drink for drink all through the night.

The whisky bottle never emptied, and Annie lost track of time. The water around them began to lighten, and Annie assumed it was somewhere near dawn. She drained her cup and set it on the table, expecting the Fisherman to refill it. No whiskey poured. Annie looked through her bleary eyes and saw that the Fisherman had slid out of his seat and was snoring happily on the floor of the cave with half a cup of whiskey still sitting on the table. Annie grabbed his shoulder to shake him awake.

"I won, I won," she slurred. "Gimme my soul."

The Fisherman tried to swat Annie's hand away, but she kept shaking him.

"Alright, alright, lemme alone." The Fisherman stood and stumbled to the wall of the cave and flipped open the door of one of the crab pots. "Suicide maiden, 1732, off the coast of France. Her lover wouldn't acknowledge their bastard." Bright bubbles floated up from the pot, and Annie could hear a clear, sweet voice repeat over and over again as the bubbles floated away, "Thank you."

"No," Annie cried. "Charlie, my brother! I came here for Charlie!"

"You never said what soul you wanted, now get gone with you." The Fisherman gestured at Annie, and the current returned, sucking her out of the cave. In moments, her head broke the water of the harbor. The sun was rising, and the air was clear. Annie gasped for breath, then swam for the dock.

It took Annie three days to recover from the hangover caused by the Fisherman's whiskey. For those three days, she haunted the Inner Harbor in search of the Witch. On the evening of the third day, Annie despaired of ever finding a way to return to the Fisherman's lair, and she sat on the edge of the dock in the sunset light and cried.

"I gather things didn't go so well," said a familiar voice behind her. The Witch settled herself down next to Annie.

"He let loose the wrong soul." Annie snuffled. "I was so drunk I forgot to ask for Charlie specifically. Why didn't you tell me to set the terms before we started?"

"Well," said the Witch. "I would think that would be pretty obvious. You can't expect the old goat to play fair, now can you?"

"I need to go back," Annie said. "I have to get Charlie out. The nightmares are getting worse."

"I figured as much." The Witch produced another vial from her voluminous carpet bag. "Same rules as last time. Hopefully, you learned from your mistakes."

The Witch left Annie on the dock where she paced back and forth, impatient for midnight.

When the little hand clicked into position over the 12, Annie tore into the vial and was in the water in seconds. The current sucked her down again and dropped her in front of the Fisherman's cave. Annie ran inside.

"Fisherman!" she shouted. "I challenge you!"

"You again," he muttered from the shadows. "Didn't you get enough last time?"

"I didn't get the soul I came for. Do you accept my challenge?"

"Fine, fine. I haven't got anything better to do. Let's get on with it."

This time, the Fisherman produced a bottle of bourbon from under his sail cloth and began to pour the drinks. Once again, the potion afforded Annie some protection, and as the water lightened, the Fisherman was snoring on the floor of the cave. Annie shook him awake again.

"No tricks this time," she slurred. "A drowned boy, you know who I want." The Fisherman shambled across the cave and flipped open another crab pot.

"Drowned boy, 1561, off the coast of Ireland; his stepmother wanted her son to inherit the family fortune." He cackled.

"No!" Annie cried as the current sucked her away again. As she surfaced in the harbor, the Fisherman's parting words rang in her head.

"You never said which drowned boy."

Annie got ticketed for loitering four times before the Witch showed up again.

"Forgot to set the terms again?" The Witch sat on the bench next to Annie.

"Just one more vial," Annie begged. "Please just give me one more vial. I'll get it right this time."

"You'll have to," said the Witch. "This is the last time you can have the potion. If you take it a fourth time, you'll be dead before you hit the water."

"I promise I'll get it right this time. Just give it to me, please."

The Witch produced the vial, and Annie snatched it from her hands.

"Same rules, last chance," the Witch said over her shoulder as she melted into the afternoon crowd.

When midnight came again, Annie took the potion and was in the water for the last time; the raging current pulled her through the sea and dropped her at the Fisherman's door. The water didn't even finish swirling before she entered the cave.

"You again?" the Fisherman said from the shadows before Annie could speak. "What are you, a glutton for punishment? Alcoholic perhaps?"

"I'm challenging you again, Fisherman," said Annie. "But this time, let's get the prize straight before we start drinking."

"Sure, fine," said the Fisherman. "I've got plenty of Charlies to spare... several hundred, in fact."

"I don't want just one soul this time, Fisherman. I want them all. This time, if I win you have to let all the souls go free."

"That's quite a prize." His eyes narrowed. "But what's in it for me, my pretty young thing? What do I get if I win?"

"What do you want?"

"I think you know what I want," said the Fisherman. "It gets awful cold and lonely in this cave all by myself, surrounded by the dead."

"Just tell me what you want."

"If I win, you'll spend the rest of forever in this cave with me."

"Done," said Annie. "What do we drink this time? Scotch...vodka?"

"Oh no, a special wager calls for a special drink." The Fisherman hobbled to the back of the cave and returned rolling a cask almost as big as he was. "I have here a cask of most magical wine, wrung from the blood of the sailors who died."

Annie turned pale, and the cave swayed around her.

"No backing out now, girlie."

The Fisherman settled in his accustomed spot and produced the cups from under his sail cloth. Annie swallowed hard and took her place. She had no idea if the potion offered any protection from magical blood wine.

The potion didn't offer as much protection from the blood wine as it had from the other drinks. Annie began to feel woozy after the third cup. She knew she needed to do something sneaky or else she would be the Fisherman's prisoner forever, and Charlie would still be stuck in a crab pot. They were on their fifth cup when she noticed that hers was nearly full, and his was nearly empty.

"Are you sure that pot up there is latched tight? I think one of your souls is escaping." Annie pointed to a pot high on the wall behind the Fisherman. While his back was turned, she switched the cups.

"Nah, it's fine. You need to get your eyes checked, girlie." The Fisherman drained the cup in one gulp. When the eighth cup came, Annie tried the same trick again.

"Are you sure it's latched tight? I could swear I see one of them wiggling out," she said.

Once again, when his back was turned, Annie switched the cups. When he turned back, the Fisherman eyed the cups suspiciously.

"You wouldn't be trying to trick me now, girlie, would you?"

"Now, why would I do that? You've tricked me so many times, you've got to be smarter than me. It would be useless to even try to fool you."

"True," he said and drained the cup.

He filled them again, and they began another round, and then another. Annie noticed the water lightening around her and knew that dawn could not be far off. She tried the trick one last time.

"I saw one escape! I swear! It's floating away over there." Annie pointed to the wall behind the Fisherman, and once more, while his back was turned, she switched the cups.

"Damn, girl." He growled as he drained his cup. "You must be blind. There's nothing there." Slamming his cup back on the table, he began to sway. He tried to settle back into his chair, and instead, he slid to the floor and began to snore.

The current came swooping into the cave, and the very walls shook from its force. The crab pots rattled in their places, and one by one, each door snicked open. The spirits bubbled out, trilling their joy at their freedom. Thousands of voices in dozens of languages and dozens more dialects joined in a chorus of ecstasy. The magic current carried Annie home one last time wrapped in the gratitude of drowned souls. As each one slid past her she felt a little of their stories: a sailor from the British Navy who fell overboard in a gale, a Japanese girl who had thrown herself off a seaside cliff to her death rather than shame her family when she did not get into university, and then, there was Charlie.

Annie felt the warmth of her little brother's heart as his soul drifted past on his way to heaven. She felt his love and pride in his big sister. She felt peace settling into her heart at long last.

As her head broke the water in the harbor, she felt hands grabbing her ankles. Strong hands yanked her under the water again. Looking down, she saw the Fisherman with his burning green eye with his hands wrapped around her ankles. Annie kicked hard and caught him in the face. He let go, and she swam like mad for the docks. Just as she reached the ladder, she felt his hands on her ankles again. He was strong, and Annie was losing her grip on the slick metal ladder. Just as he was about to pull her under again, two hands reached down and hauled her up out of the water and out of the Fisherman's grip. It was the Witch.

"Damn, girl," she said. "You can't do anything on your own, can you?"

They heard the Fisherman bellow below. "No fair! No fair!"

Annie and the Witch lay on their bellies and peeked over the edge of the dock.

"You helped her... no fair! Do you realize how long it took me to collect those souls?"

"Five hundred thirty-three years, nine months, and eleven days, but who's counting?" said the Witch.

"Give 'em back!" The Fisherman slapped the water.

"Why don't you come back to the cottage, and we'll talk about it?" the Witch said coyly as she tossed her old gray curls.

"Why don't you come to my cave, and we'll talk about it?" said the Fisherman.

"You know the water makes my arthritis act up," said the Witch.

"Bugger off then," said the Fisherman, and he disappeared under the waves.

"Well, if you have any more relatives drown, come see me. I'll get that old goat out of his cave yet." The Witch sighed as she heaved herself to her feet.

The Witch disappeared before Annie could say a word and left her shivering on the dock in the dawn light. Annie went home to blissful, dreamless sleep.

# The Boogeyman Accords

A little girl's shriek tore through the air at 2:00 a.m. Her parents' eyes flung open, and they both groaned. They held their breath for a moment hoping it would stop, but then, another shriek came.

"Whose turn is it?" Grant mumbled through the hands clapped across his face.

"I will do anything if you will just go," moaned Sharon.

"Anything?" Grant peered through his fingers.

"Pervert," Sharon swung her legs over the side of the bed, but she was smiling as she belted her robe.

"Gracie, honey, it's okay. Mommy's coming," she called as she started to shuffle down the hall, yawning. In her head, she was already calculating how long it usually took to get Grace calmed down, then how long it would take her to get back to sleep herself, and then how long it would be before her alarm rang. It would definitely be a double espresso morning.

As usual, Grace was backed up against the headboard of her bed, knees tight to her chest and blankets drawn up to her chin. Dirty blonde hair stuck out in all directions, and her small ears and face were bright red from screaming. Her almond-shaped eyes were glued to the corner of her room closest to her closet door, and she was drawing in the breath to scream again.

"Gracie, honey, it's okay. Mommy's here." Sharon shuffled toward the bed with her arms outstretched.

Gracie just screeched again and pointed into the corner. Sharon turned her head without thinking, not expecting to see a thing in the corner of her daughter's pink bedroom. So the silent man standing in the corner with his head bowed and his hands clasped in front of him shocked her. Sharon drew in a breath and shrieked as she jumped away from the man and grabbed for her daughter, trying to pull her out of bed.

The man lifted his head, and from under the shadow of his broad-brimmed black hat, Sharon could see the thin ghost of a smile but not much else. He was swathed in a long, black cape with a high collar that hid most of his body, and he was tall.

"As gratifying as your fear is," he said, his voice was thick and low. "I'm afraid I'm not here for that."

"Get the hell out of my house!" screamed Sharon.

She heard footfalls racing down the hall, and Grant skidded into the room and put himself between the strange man and his wife and daughter.

"Who are you? What the hell do you want?" Grant demanded.

The tall, dark man bowed to the family. "I am Babau, and I have come to renew the Accords. If you'll join me outside, we'll try to resolve this quickly."

Babau took two steps toward the bedroom door, but Grant blocked his way and shoved him in the chest with both hands. Babau barely moved. He reached out and grabbed the collar of Grant's t-shirt with one hand and casually threw him over his right shoulder and into the closet doors. The closet doors collapsed under the weight, and Grant slid to the floor, stunned.

"I do hope you'll be more reasonable," Babau turned to face Sharon. She caught the glimmer of what looked like red eyes in the deep shadow of Babau's hat. "Come along."

Sharon grunted a little as she hoisted Grace onto her hip; she was small for a nine-year-old, but she was still verging on too heavy to carry. The girl twined her arms around her mother's neck and sobbed into her shoulder. Without thinking, Sharon patted her back and made soothing sounds as she followed the dark man down the hall and out of the house in a daze. Grant picked himself up from the wreckage with a groan and caught his breath, then scuttled after his wife.

Babau led them out of the house and down the street to the small tot lot where all the neighborhood children played when it was daylight. Everyone avoided it at night. As safe as their insular little neighborhood was, it still skirted some of the rougher neighborhoods in Baltimore, and it was not wise to tempt either fate or drug dealers. Waiting for Babau, Sharon, and Grant were a cast of shadowy figures that eventually resolved themselves into a tight knot of parents and children around the park benches on the edge of the lot, and monsters hanging on the monkey bars and swings. They were not monsters in a metaphorical sense, they were absolutely real monsters: claws, razor sharp teeth and all. Each one was different, and Sharon's instincts warred with each other, avoiding looking at the horror where her daughter had just played that afternoon or staring at the wide array of sinister menace waiting for her. Sharon and Grant joined the other parents and children. Everyone was in their pajamas and shivered in terrified silence.

Some of the monsters bowed to Babau and kissed the hem of his cloak. Others gave him deferential nod, which he returned. Babau clasped his hands behind his back and treaded slowly in a line between the monsters and parents, head bowed. Off in the distance, a siren wailed.

Babau stopped pacing and lifted his head just a bit. "I suppose you are all wondering why we gathered you here," he addressed the parents.

They glanced at each other and nodded timidly.

"As your children are well aware, and as you were aware before the world beat the sense of magic and wonder out of you," Babau began in deep and sonorous tones. "Monsters in the closet are real. Boogeymen exist."

The children whimpered and huddled closer to their parents. The parents clutched their children and murmured to each other about how this could possibly be true.

"We are banned from physically harming your children so long as they are biddable. We may only frighten them when they are well behaved, and if they are ill-behaved, we must follow certain protocols before we snatch them. So say the Accords."

Several of the children began to sob.

"But the Accords must be renewed every hundred years. And unless you," Babau gestured with his hand to the collected parents. "Renew the Accords, boogeymen worldwide will have no such restrictions upon them, and they will harvest your children at will."

The parents gasped, and the children wailed, and they all turned to each other talking at once. Finally, Grant's voice cut through the gabble.

"What do we have to do to renew the Accords?"

"It's very simple," said Babau. "You give us one of your children."

"Absolutely not!" roared a balding man in the back of the cluster. "I'm not giving you my kid, and I don't think anyone else will, either."

Babau cocked his head to the side and listened to the murmurs of assent. "You would put all of the world's children in danger to save one child? That's something I would expect from my own kind, not yours."

"What happens to the child? I mean, if we gave you a child?" asked a painfully thin woman with mousy brown hair.

One of the more chitenous monsters hanging on the monkey bars giggled and said, "Oh, the sacrifice is just lovely. The blood..."

"That's enough, Dokebi." Babau held his hand up to the creature. "They don't need to know our ways."

The parents looked at each other with bloodless faces, shaking their heads. "We can't do it. We can't sacrifice our own children," cried another voice from the back.

"It is very simple," said Babau. "You have three days to decide which of your children will come with us and never return home. If you do not give a child on the third night, the Accords are broken, and the boogeymen of the world will do as they choose. They will continue in this way until the sacrifice is made."

"Why us?" said the balding man. "Why are we responsible for renewing the Accords?"

Babau shrugged. "Every time the Accords are to be renewed, we approach a different people. It was simply your turn."

"But..." The man drew in his breath to protest, but in between one breath and the next, Babau and his monsters vanished.

The next afternoon, after everyone had gone to work and come home, the parents gathered in Sharon and Grant's kitchen to talk. The children were all sent to the basement rec room to play, and the parents clutched mugs of coffee and watched each other from shadowed eyes.

Grant heaved a great sigh. "So, what are we going to do?"

"Well, I'm not giving them my kid, that's for sure," said one of the fathers, and he was echoed by a chorus of "me neither" from around the room.

"But what about the threats? He said they'd kidnap and kill children all over the world."

"Oh, come on, Grant," said Morty, the kitchen light reflecting over the balding top of his head. "You can't take that whacko at face value. They are obviously just a bunch of human thugs in really good costumes trying to get a hold of our kids for who knows what kind of twisted shit. The Boogeyman is not real."

Parents around the room nodded in agreement.

"So," said Grant. "We do nothing?"

"We do nothing."

And so it was on the third night that Babau and his monsters came to the tot lot at the agreed upon hour and found it empty. He scanned the windows of the surrounding homes and found them all dark. The humans had no intention of bringing the proper sacrifice.

"Go." He growled and waved his hands at the monsters arrayed around him. "The Accords are broken."

The next morning, parents around the world woke to thousands of reports of terrorized and missing children all over the globe, but only a small group of them in Southeast Baltimore knew what was really behind the spike in crime against children. They met again in Sharon and Grant's kitchen, the children packed away downstairs and sleepy afternoon sunlight streaming through the cheerful yellow curtains. No one would meet each other's eyes, and everyone's cups of coffee grew cold in their hands.

"We have to do something," Grant said, breaking the silence. "We can't let it keep going on like this."

"I don't know what we can do," said Morty. "I'm not going to give away my son like a lamb to slaughter, and I can't very well ask any of you to do it, either."

"How long do you think it will be before one of our kids disappears anyway?" Sharon's voice was tight and sharp. "Babau said that if the Accords got broken, all bets were off. They could be coming for our children any night. We could lose all of them instead of just one."

Around the room, eyes widened and jaws dropped open. No one had thought of that.

"So, how do we decide? Do we draw straws or play rock, paper, scissors or something?"

"Be serious, Morty," said Sharon.

"I am being serious!" he said. "I really don't know what's the fairest way to make one of use lose a kid."

"I have an idea." A chunky brown-skinned woman raised her hand a bit, her voice shy. All eyes turned to her, and she swallowed hard and twisted in her seat. "We could give them Grace."

"What?" Sharon and Grant choked in shock. Sharon was the first to recover her voice. "Why our daughter, Denise? You offered her up pretty quick." Sharon's eyes narrowed, and Grant continued to sputter.

"Well," Denise said, twisting her hands in her lap and looking around the room for support. "It's just that, well, she's retarded. It's not like she's going to cure cancer or anything. At least all of our kids have a chance to grow up and make something of themselves."

"My daughter is worth just as much as any one of your kids," Sharon's voice came out in a hiss. "Yes, she has Down Syndrome, but she's very high functioning. Maybe she won't become a doctor or a lawyer, but she's got just as much to give as anyone. Her life is just as precious as anyone's." Sharon's enraged eyes swept the room, and no one would meet her gaze, least of all Denise.

The room was silent for a long moment, then burst into loud shouts as each parent argued for sons and daughters. Completely unnoticed, little Grace perched on the top of the basement stairs, listening to it all from behind the cracked door. The other children had tossed her out of their games, and she had nowhere else to go.

The next morning, Sharon began to shuffle through her routine: making coffee, going to wake her daughter. But Grace's bed was empty. She ripped the blankets off and did not find her daughter playfully scrunched at the bottom and giggling. The girl wasn't under the bed or in the closet either.

"Grant!" she called with desperation in her voice as she ran back down the hall to their bedroom.

Sharon and Grant scoured the neighborhood and didn't find a trace of Grace anywhere. As they passed her house, Denise was stepping out onto her porch, dressed for work and arguing with her son about his undone homework. Denise took in Sharon and Grant's wild eyes and their hoarse voices all at once. She sucked in her breath and pulled her son close, her dark complexion ashen.

"It's started," Sharon said as they passed by, her voice bitter.

That evening, the parents gathered at the tot lot to wait for Babau and his entourage. They had no idea how they were going to decide which child to hand over, and they held their children close and murmured everything they didn't want to leave unsaid as they waited.

They waited for a long time, until dawn, in fact. Babau and the monsters never showed. The parents looked at each other, mystified, and carried their sleeping children home. They all checked the news and found that during the night not a single child had been abducted, and the thousands who had disappeared had reappeared in their beds, safe and sound. But Grace's bed remained empty; she was still nowhere to be found.

Sharon and Grant called the police and reported their daughter missing. The officers were kind and concerned as they talked to Sharon and Grant and were thorough as they interviewed the rest of the neighborhood residents. They could find no evidence of foul play, no jimmied locks or broken windows, no strange fingerprints. They promised to keep Sharon and Grant informed and that they would do everything in their power to bring Grace home. But it didn't take them long to bring the couple an answer they didn't want to hear.

An officer came to their house about suppertime carrying a small digital tablet. He showed them footage from the city camera mounted on the street light near the tot lot. The city had installed it in an effort to identify the drug dealers using the lot as a base of operations. The grainy black-and-white video showed their daughter walking to the tot lot, having a conversation with the air, then taking the hand of someone who didn't exist, and walking out of range of the camera. Grant turned his head away, and Sharon put a hand over her mouth and sobbed.

"I'm sorry," said the officer. "It appears that your daughter wandered off on her own. We're still doing everything we can to find her."

Grant thanked the officer and showed him out while his wife Sharon stared into space with her hand still over her mouth.

Later in the evening, in their own bedroom, Sharon paced and seethed as Grant watched her from the bed. "I can't believe this is happening. If he was just going to take a child in the first place, why didn't he just do it? What was the point of all that build up?"

"I don't know," said Grant.

She went to their closet and wrenched the door open. "Babau!" she screamed into the ranks of neatly hung pants and oxford shirts. "I want answers! Where is my daughter?"

The closet was silent. Sharon waited, then tears began to trickle down her cheeks, and she sobbed. She turned away from the closet with her face in her hands. Grant took her in his arms.

"What kind of answers do you want?" came a rich, deep voice from the closet. The couple gasped and turned to see Babau unfolding himself from the darkness.

"I want to know where my daughter is. I want to know why you took her." Sharon sobbed.

"Your daughter is ours now. And we did not take her," said Babau.

"How? What? I don't understand. What about the Accords?" Grant pulled his wife closer, his voice cracking.

"What about the Accords?" Babau said. "They have been renewed. They were signed, and the sacrifice was given."

"I didn't give you my daughter!" Sharon shouted and tried to pull out of her husband's embrace.

"No," Babau said as he smiled, revealing a mouth full of needle-sharp teeth. "But she gave herself, and all that was needed was a human to sign in proxy for all of humanity."

Sharon's brow furrowed, and she shook her head from side to side. "But she's only a child... she can't sign a contract."

"As long as the human is of sound mind and body, any human can sign the Accords," Babau said as he bowed to them both and stepped back to the closet. "But now I must bid you adieu. I do have my appointed rounds with naughty children to fulfill." And with that, he was gone.

Three nights later, the closet door in Sharon and Grant's bedroom opened without a sound. A small figure crept forth and crossed the room to perch on the footboard and watch them sleep. Their breath went in and out in a steady rhythm, but their brows showed deep lines of sorrow and worry.

"I'm sorry," Grace whispered and was surprised to hear her voice come in a soft, sibilant cadence. She held her hands up to the moonlight from the window and looked in wonder at the iridescent green scales that covered her skin and the barbed claws at the end of each finger instead of the smooth pale skin and translucent fingernails she remembered from before. Taking in the sights of the once familiar bedroom with her much better reptilian eyes, she sighed.

Grace's head came around at the creak of a floorboard in front of the closet. Babau stood there with his head bowed and his hands folded in front of him.

"Are you ready?" his voice was as gentle as a summer breeze on Grace's new ears.

She looked at her parents wistfully again. "I really can't let them know that I'm alright?"

"No," said Babau. "You are no longer one of them. You are one of us, and we must keep our people separated." He held his arms out to the new, young boogeyman.

Grace went to him, and he enfolded her in tender arms and kissed the top of her head. Even though the transformation had given her a good eight inches of additional height, the top of her head still barely came to the middle of Babau's chest.

"It is difficult to cross over," he said. "We all understand that, but there are compensations to living this life, child."

"Like what?" Grace said, tilting her head up so she could look into Babau's red eyes.

"Remember all those children who treated you poorly when you were human? The ones who made fun of you and called you names?"

Grace nodded, and Babau smiled, showing his wicked needle teeth.

"You see," he said. "Such treatment is the mark of a naughty child, and it is the pleasure, nay, the duty of the boogeyman to ensure that they are properly punished."

Grace smiled, showing her brand new gleaming fangs, and Babau began to back into the closet, holding her hand and lightly drawing her with him. She spared one last backward glance to Sharon and Grant, then stepped over the threshold into the darkness of the closet.

# Reynolds and the Demon

A slender man in a disheveled suit, his hair sprouting wildly in all directions, stumbled through the empty, moonlit streets of Baltimore, waving his hands over his head, alternately mumbling and shouting.

"You can't have it, Reynolds," he muttered as he turned in place in the middle of the street, scanning the sky. "You said I could have it." He pouted and shoved his hands in his pockets, sidestepping a cold pile of horse manure as he wandered on.

A raven peeked out from behind the gable of a roof and watched the meandering figure with a gimlet eye. When the man did not turn and notice him, the bird ghosted down on silent black feathers to perch on the sign advertising a pub, closed at this late hour.

The man heard the iron bolts squeal as the sign swung under the weight of the bird, and he whirled around and shook his fists in the air.

"You said it was mine, Reynolds," he shouted. "You can't have it back." He was breathing hard, and his face was angry red.

The bird merely cocked his head to the side and blinked. Man and bird stood like that, frozen in an unlikely tableau, until the man broke off his stare.

"Bah!" He waved his hands at the raven and turned to march further up the street. The bird called after him, but the man just waved his hand behind him and kept walking.

The raven took wing again and this time alighted on the sign for a cooper's shop, also closed, far ahead of the meandering man. He watched the man with sharp, black eyes as he approached with his hands tucked under his arms and his eyes trained on the ground, mumbling to himself. The man was nearly upon him when the bird called out to him again.

The man startled and cried out, turning his eyes upward. "Damn you, Reynolds! You almost gave me a heart attack."

The bird called out again, but softly this time.

"But I can't give it back." The man held his hands up imploringly. "I need it. You'd kill me if you took it."

The bird shook his head and cawed again.

"I won't let you," the man cried and twisted around, taking off running in the direction he'd come from.

The raven waited a moment and then took off from his perch with a strong downbeat of his wings. He caught up to the running man in just a few wing beats and dove down with a neat folding of his wings, striking the man in his right shoulder making him stumble and fall to the ground. The man rolled over on his back and raised up his hands to ward off the bird, who had winged back skyward only to turn quickly and dive back toward the man again.

The raven hovered over him, picking at the cuffs of his suit and his shirt with his talons, cawing all the while.

"No, no, no!" screamed the man. "I won't! I won't give it back."

The man rolled to his side and curled into a fetal ball, using his arms to wrap around and protect his head. The bird gripped his shoulder, pecking down at his face. The man kept his lips sealed in a tight, white line and tried to wrap his arms even tighter even as he shook his head back and forth. Then, the raven clamped his beak down on the man's thumb, causing him to cry out in pain. This was just what the bird had been waiting for.

The raven lunged forward into the man's mouth and plucked out a small, swirling red ball, barely larger than a child's marble. As soon as he had it in his beak, the bird launched skyward, flying hard and fast. The man rolled to his knees and shook his fists at the quickly disappearing bird.

"You're a bastard, Reynolds!" he screamed. "This is going to kill me!"

The man did die four days later, on October 7, 1849, at Washington College Hospital.

Jenny was trudging up Fayette Street when she saw the big black bird hop-stepping with his wings spread around the base of the Poe monument at the Westminster church on the corner of Fayette and Green. She drew closer, her hands tucked in the pockets of her hoodie sweatshirt, trying to see what had the bird's attention. It was obviously hunting something, but Jenny didn't think there was a lot to interest a big bird like a raven in a graveyard. She rested her hands on the iron fence that surrounded the cemetery and peered in.

The raven stood with his back to her on the brick surrounding the marble monument to one of Baltimore's treasured sons. His wings were flared out, his head was lowered, and he was trying to threaten something in front of him. Jenny went to her tip-toes to try to catch a glimpse what had the bird so angry. She still couldn't see. The bird cawed and jumped once to the left, apparently to counter his opponent. Jenny bit her bottom lip and paused. If she went in through the open wrought iron gate just to her left, she might scare the bird away, as well as his prey. But what could a bird be hunting in a churchyard paved over with bricks?

Jenny stepped through the gate slowly, placing each sneakered foot with care. The raven never noticed her as he was so focused on the prey in front of him. She kept sidling around until she could see what the bird was trying to catch. Finally, she could see what so fascinated the big, black bird.

It was a small, swirling red ball, barely larger than a child's marble. Jenny felt the hair on her arms and back of her neck stand on end, and her throat constricted. She might not know exactly what it was, but she had some ideas. It was definitely dark magic of some sort, and it was strong. There was no way Jenny was going to let something like that stand in her city. She put too much effort into keeping the magic in Baltimore safe for magical and non-magical creatures alike. She took a step toward the ball and bird stand-off, her fists clenched by her side. That was when the raven noticed her.

He cawed out, the sound echoing all over the churchyard, and put himself between her and the glowing ball. This time the lowered head, flared wings, and open beak were for her.

"Crap," she muttered as she tried to sidestep around the bird with no luck. "Damn bird, get out of my way." She flapped her arms at it, hoping to scare it away, and instead, he just flapped his wings back at her.

The glowing ball started to roll for the open iron gate while Jenny and the bird danced from side to side, trying to get around each other. Both Jenny and the raven saw it out of the corner of their eyes and lunged for it at the same moment. The raven pounced faster than Jenny and clutched the ball tight in both talons. He sank around it, crouching over it like an egg, and his wings drooped. Jenny could have sworn she heard the bird groan.

"That's a nice birdie," she said in as soothing a voice as she could manage and crouched down, then reached out to try to get the ball from under the bird. "That's not something you need. Let me have it."

The bird snapped at her reaching hand, and she drew back just in time to avoid a nasty bite. He opened his beak and hissed. Jenny raised an eyebrow.

"I'm getting the feeling you're not like your ordinary brothers, are you?" she said, rubbing her nearly wounded hand.

The raven nodded and let his head drop to his chest.

"Do you have any idea what that is that you're sitting on?"

The raven lifted his head and nodded again.

"And you were just trying to keep me from getting hurt?

He nodded yet again to her question.

"Well," she said. "That's not really something you need to worry about, birdman. I'm a witch, and I do know a thing or two about handling magical objects."

The bird made a blatant show of looking her up and down with a skeptical eye, her obvious Asian ancestry in combination with sneakers, jeans, t-shirt, and a hooded sweatshirt topped off by a coal black bob with hot pink streaks tipped in purple.

"What? I'm not allowed to adapt to the times? I'm always supposed to wear a kimono?" She sighed and rubbed the bridge of her nose. "Look, I can help you. Do you want me to or not?"

The raven stared at her for a long minute, and then nodded. Jenny slipped off her sweatshirt to wrap around him and gathered him up. They stepped out onto the sidewalk and became just one more of the usual unusual sights on the street in Baltimore as Jenny hot-footed it home with the raven tucked under her arm.

Once they reached her book-lined basement apartment three blocks away, Jenny settled the bird on the couch and started to rummage through flat plastic storage bins stored under her bed on the far side of the room, partially hidden by gauzy blue curtains.

"Ah-ha!" She came up with a clear glass box about the size of a deck of cards, bound on its edges and corners with copper. Each face of the box was etched with esoteric symbols that dipped and swirled with reckless abandon. She brought it to the raven and unwrapped the sweatshirt enough for him to move.

"It's only temporary," she said as she sat on the edge of the coffee table, flipped open the lid and held it out to the bird. "I know something like this isn't strong enough to hold something like that for very long." She nodded to the swirling marble. "But it would give us a chance to talk and give you at least a little break."

The bird paused, and Jenny could have sworn he sighed. He rose up on one leg, gripping the marble tight in his other talon and dropped it in the box. Jenny snapped the lid shut and twisted the hasp. Gasping, she almost dropped the box onto her oak coffee table but managed not to break it. She shook her hands and blew on her fingertips.

"Man, that thing's got some heat."

The bird ruffled his feathers and cawed softly.

Jenny crossed her arms across her chest and cocked her head at the bird. "And now that we've got a little wiggle room, we need to figure out a way to chat. Wait right there."

The bird watched her with curiosity as she dug through more plastic tubs, deeper ones this time, stored in the lower cabinets of her kitchen. Ten minutes and three tubs later, Jenny crowed victory again and held up a small glass tube of deep gray powder that sparkled ever so slightly in the dim afternoon sun that came through her high half-windows. There wasn't much.

"Just a little hoodoo I got from a root doctor friend down in New Orleans." She waggled the vial and resumed her seat on the coffee table. "There isn't much, but I think it's enough to give us a bit of conversation."

She worked out the cork stopper with a gentle hand and paused. "Do I have your permission?"

The bird nodded and sat up a little straighter on his sweatshirt nest.

"Here we go, cross your feathers," she said under her breath and dipped her finger into the vial. The words that came from her mouth sounded like a strange amalgam of French, Afrikaans, and Latin. The music of the language twisted her lips, and she smeared the gray powder all around the bird's beak, dipping her finger back into the vial whenever necessary, tracing strange symbols, top, bottom, and sides. The powder ran out, and she fell silent, sitting back expectantly with the empty vial and her hands in her lap.

At first, nothing happened, then the bird hacked once and groaned. This time, Jenny was sure she wasn't imagining the humanity to his groan.

"I'll never understand how you don't hurt yourselves when you speak," the raven said in a clear, cultured voice. "Normal vocal cords just weren't meant to work that way."

"Maybe not normal bird vocal cords." Jenny laughed. "But it's just fine for human vocal cords."

"Pah," said the bird and ruffled his feathers all over.

"First things first." Jenny clapped her hands together. "What should I call you? Do you have a name?"

"He always called me Reynolds, so I suppose that would do just fine." His voice was soft and wistful, and he wouldn't meet Jenny's eyes.

"Who called you Reynolds?"

"The one I couldn't save," Reynolds hid his beak under his wing, causing his voice came out muffled. "The one I damned. Do we really have to do this?"

"I think we do. I have to know what I'm dealing with or this could go very, very wrong."

Reynolds sighed and pulled his head out from under his wing. "That thing that I'm holding is a productivity demon with a taste for artists. It goads them to create and create, going without sleep or food or drink unless someone forces them to stop, which usually doesn't last. It will make them keep going until they kill themselves either through starvation or exhaustion, then it moves along to another host."

"Is that what happened to your friend?" Jenny's voice was soft with concern.

The bird shook his head and sighed. "No, that one was all my fault. I'd been caring for the demon for almost a century when Edgar asked me if he could just hold it a while. He promised that he'd give it back as soon as I asked him to. And I was just so damn tired from holding the demon that long that I agreed.

"He wrote and wrote, and it was beautiful, and it seemed like he was strong enough to handle the demon. He still ate and slept, still spent time with his family and friends. But I was convinced that it was all an elaborate show for my benefit, and I asked for the demon back. When he wouldn't give the demon back, I was convinced that I was right and needed to take it away by force. He told me that it would kill him, but I didn't listen. I took the demon away, and he was right. He died four days later." Reynolds sunk down and hung his head.

"Did you ever try to give it to another writer to see if it would work again? Maybe writers are just a hardier breed of artist?"

Reynolds nodded. "But it drove Howard mad. I was wrong again. I took it from the man who could handle it, and I gave it to the one who couldn't."

"Have you ever considered locking the thing up in something stronger?"

"Of course I have!" Reynolds shouted in a bitter voice, flaring out his wings. "I haven't carried this cursed demon for centuries because I'm stupid." He settled back down. "I know what I need to do, but I don't have the hands to do it with."

Jenny brightened up with a huge smile and held up her hands and waggled her fingers. "Well, now you do. Jenny the witch, at your service. I'll be your hands."

The demon marble rolled around the glass box, faster and faster around the edges, slowly walking toward the edge of the coffee table. Jenny frowned and pushed it back to the center of the table with a finger. The marble pulsed and glowed with hot, red light, almost as if annoyed.

"First things first," Jenny said. "Do we need to do the ritual by the full moon or dark moon?"

Reynolds opened his beak to speak but all that came out was a harsh caw.

It was Jenny's turn to sigh. "Damn, well, at least we got some time." She held up her hands, palms out. "My left for the dark moon and my right for the full moon."

Reynolds tapped her left hand with his beak without hesitation.

"Good," she said. "Do we need to lock it in something made of natural substance or man made? Man made my left, natural my right."

Reynolds cocked his head to the side and considered the question, then he quickly tapped both hands.

Jenny bit her lip. "Oh, this is going to be a tough one. Ok, lots of ingredients left or just few right."

Reynolds tapped her left hand.

"Alrighty then." Jenny slapped her hands on her thighs and glanced at the demon marble in the box, sitting still in the center of the table glowering at them both. "It looks like it's going to sulk for a while, so why don't you come into the kitchen and show me what we'll need out of my stocks, then we'll make up a shopping list."

Reynolds bobbed his head up and down and accepted her hand up onto her shoulder.

"We'd better move fast. We only have three days to full dark."

The last of the herbs burnt out and sent tendrils of pungent smoke into the dark night sky. Jenny straightened up from her squat and leaned back to stretch her back muscles.

"Damn, I think we did it, Reynolds."

Reynolds hopped around her feet, wings spread, cawing with joy. Jenny bent over and picked up the heartwood fountain pen from the makeshift altar she'd spread out on the ground by Poe's grave, natural wood plus man made nib covered Reynolds' requirements. She sniffed it and held it up to the weak starlight.

"I can still smell the demon, but it doesn't burn like before." She grinned and looked down at Reynolds. "We totally did it! How about a celebratory dinner?"

Reynolds bobbed his head up and down and cawed loudly. Jenny tucked the pen in her purse and gathered up all her ritual gear before anyone came to investigate the strange noises or smells. Everything seemed to be going just fine, until a few days later.

Jenny was in the kitchen trying to keep Reynolds out of the carrot she was slicing for her salad when her friend Bobby came for a visit.

He flopped on her couch and moaned. "I'm so blocked! And no one understands me."

She poked her head out of the kitchen. "You know, just because no one understands you doesn't make you an artist. Sometimes, it just means you're a weirdo."

"You're not helping." Bobby threw a throw pillow at her, but he was laughing, his even white teeth flashing against his ebony dark skin. "Say something funny or inspirational. Isn't that what artist's friends are supposed to be good for?"

Jenny struck a dramatic pose with her hands on her hips in the kitchen doorway. "It was a dark and stormy night..." She dodged as he threw another pillow at her.

"Hey, that was funny!" she called from the kitchen.

Bobby rolled his eyes. "You would think with all the weird shit that goes on around here that I'd have plenty to write about."

"Well," said Jenny, returning to chopping her carrot. "Instead of focusing on the weird shit that won't come to you, why don't you write about the ordinary shit that happens to everyone? People could relate, ya know."

Bobby stretched his legs out, put his hands behind his head and stared up at the ceiling. The rhythmic sound of Jenny's chef knife in the kitchen counted off the seconds. A light exploded in Bobby's eyes.

"Can I borrow a pen?" he called.

"Sure," Jenny said. "There's a cup full of them on the desk in my bedroom."

"No time," Bobby muttered, and he started hunting through Jenny's purse on the coffee table. The heartwood fountain pen nearly leaped into his hand. He grabbed a crumpled old grocery list out of her purse at the same time and scribbled a line on the back. He paused, looked at the pen in his hand, and then filled up the rest of the back of the list with cramped script.

"I gotta go. I think I finally figured out a way around this block. Thanks, Jenny!" He shoved the pen and paper into his pocket and bolted for the door.

Jenny came out of the kitchen to say goodbye, but Bobby was already gone. All that was left was the echo of the slamming door. Jenny glanced back at Reynolds where he was still perched on the counter, and she shrugged and laughed.

"Artists are weird sometimes."

Jenny and Reynolds still didn't suspect anything was wrong until a couple of days later when Bobby's fiancée Pam called.

"Well, Bobby's block broke in a big way. Whatever you said to him really made a difference. Looks like I'll be a writing widow for a while." Pam laughed.

Jenny laughed with her. "I'm glad I could help. I didn't think I said anything deep, but you never know where an artist is going to take it, I guess."

"True, true." Pam sighed. "But it is kind of weird."

"What's kind of weird?"

"It used to be when Bobby was on a roll that he'd still take breaks. He said it fed the muse. But he hasn't stopped since he got back from your place. I don't think he's slept at all, and I did get him to eat something, but he almost bit off my head."

Jenny felt her stomach drop. "That doesn't sound healthy."

"Oh, it's probably nothing." Pam forced a laugh. "You know me, I'm just a natural worry wart. But I'll see you at that gallery opening Kelly was talking about?"

"Yeah, sure," Jenny's voice was far away as she drifted toward the living room and hung up the phone. Snatching her purse off the couch, she up-ended it all over the coffee table. She searched through all the flotsam and jetsam, half-empty packs of gum and crumpled receipts but couldn't find one pen. She vaulted over the back of her couch and bounded into the bedroom area and dumped her pencil cup across her desk. There were plenty of pens, but none of them were heartwood fountain pens.

She sank down onto the edge of her bed and put her head in her hands.

"Oh, crap."

Jenny stood on the sidewalk outside Bobby and Pam's row house with a bottle of wine in her hands and Reynolds perched on her shoulder.

"Okay," she said. "Here's the plan. You wait in the tree across the street until I give you the signal, then you fly in through the open window and grab the pen and fly out. Then, we find some other place to trap this beast."

Reynolds let out a short caw and launched himself into the skinny, city-planted maple across the street. Jenny took a deep breath, squared her shoulders, and marched up to the door.

"Hi! Thanks for coming." Pam welcomed Jenny with a hug. "Bobby's still working, so it'll probably be just us girls for dinner. I made carbonara."

"That sounds fantastic," Jenny said as she handed the wine to Pam. "Maybe I can get Bobby to join us."

Pam retreated to the kitchen to open the wine while Jenny made her way into the living room.

"Hey, Bobby, are you going to join us for dinner?"

Bobby grunted, hunched over a notebook with the heartwood fountain pen flying along full speed. "No time. I gotta finish this book."

"Oh, come on," Jenny wheedled. "You can take a break for some dinner. The ideas will still be there later."

Bobby's head reared back, and he looked at Jenny with the gleam of madness in his eyes. "No, they won't," he growled and turned back to the page.

Pam came out from the kitchen and handed Jenny a glass of wine. "This is what he's been like for two weeks. This is his third book."

"So, he starts stuff and doesn't finish it?" Jenny took a sip of her wine.

"Oh no, he finishes it alright... long ones, too."

Jenny raised an eyebrow. "Are they any good?"

Pam nodded. "They're great; exactly what I knew he could do if he could just buckle down and focus. But now that he's focusing so much I wish he would unfocus now and then."

"Let me try something else." Jenny crossed the room to Bobby's desk by the open front window. In a sing-song voice, she said, "I brought your favorite Chianti, Bobby."

He just grunted and waved her away without taking his eyes off the page.

"Bobby," Jenny said with a hint of steel in her voice and pushing out her will as hard as she could. "I'm not going to leave you alone until you get up from that desk and at least have a glass of wine with us."

"Will you leave me alone if I have a glass of wine with you?" He finally looked up and his hand stilled for the first time since Jenny had entered the apartment.

"Yes."

"Fine, then bring it here." Bobby held out his hand, and Pam's eyes widened in surprise. She turned and scampered into the kitchen for another glass.

"No," said Jenny, still pushing out her will. "You're going to get up from this desk, and you're going have it in the other room with us like a civilized person."

With his jaw clenched tight, Bobby threw the heartwood pen down on his open notebook and stomped across the room to where Pam stood with his glass of wine. While he wasn't looking, Jenny stuck her arm out the window and waved two fingers up and down three times. Bobby already had the wine in his hand and was drinking it down in one long gulp, locking angry eyes with Jenny over the rim of the glass.

Halfway through he dropped the glass and cried, "What the?" and tried to leap across the room when he saw Reynolds ghost in through the window and land on his desk. Jenny put herself between Bobby and Reynolds and would not move.

"Get out of my way!" he screamed, raising up his fists.

Jenny stepped aside, but it was too late for Bobby. Reynolds already had the heartwood pen in his talons and was out the window, flying straight back to Jenny's place.

"You bitch!" Bobby shouted at Jenny. "That was my lucky pen."

"Bobby!" Pam cried in shock.

Jenny was trembling slightly but not for the reason Pam thought. "Maybe I'd better go," she said.

Two months later, a much saner Bobby sprawled across Jenny's couch again.

"I don't know how to explain it," he said. "I'm so sorry for what I said, but it really was like I was possessed."

"I already told you it's okay from the last six times you apologized, Bobby. Would you stop already?" Jenny perched on the loveseat with a cup of tea. "How's the book going anyway?"

"It's slow going," groaned Bobby. "I mean, I know what I want to say, and I've got the plot all right there in my head, but it comes out so slow! At least when I was crazy I was writing faster."

"What about the ones you finished during your, umm, episode?" Jenny sipped her tea again.

"My publisher loved them!" Bobby grinned. "He's trying to rush the first one through the editing process so we can get it on the shelves for the Christmas rush, and then get the other one out in time for beach reading season."

"I'm happy for you, Bobby, really." Her eyes flicked to the bust of Pallas over her front door and Reynolds peeking out from behind it. At least Bobby would never be able to lift that out of her apartment without her noticing.

# About the Author

Michelle D. Sonnier earned her BA from University of Baltimore and her MS from Towson University. While she was at Towson, she came to realize that her stories fell flat without some element of the supernatural. So, she abandoned "high literature" and embraced genre fiction, most especially urban fantasy.

But a girl has to eat, and so she took on jobs in the cube farms of America. Even as she made her way in the world of offices and high technology in order to keep the bills paid, she never gave up on her dream of being a professional storyteller. After some successes selling single short stories to such venues as Tales of the Talisman magazine, Allegory eZine, and the anthology publisher Sam's Dot Publications, she put together the stories that became this collection.

She continues to hone her craft and is working on novels involving clockwork witches and demon fighting pirates. Michelle hopes one day to be able to write full-time, which would no doubt make her husband happy and would please two cats who would prefer her at home as much as possible to attend to can-opening and belly-rubbing duties. You can find out more about the author and all her current projects or contact her personally at www.michelledsonnier.com.